Dream Sequence

Adam Foulds

BIBLIOASIS

WINDSOR, ONTARIO

FIRST EDITION

Library and Archives Canada Cataloguing in Publication

Foulds, Adam, 1974-, author
    Dream sequence / Adam Foulds.

Issued in print and electronic formats.
ISBN 978-1-77196-281-0 (softcover).--ISBN 978-1-77196-282-7 (ebook)

    I. Title.

PS6106.O95D74 2019   823'.92   C2018-904424-1
                                                     C2018-904425-X

Readied for the press by Daniel Wells
Typeset by Chris Andrechek
Cover designed by Michel Vrana

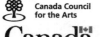

Published with the generous assistance of the Canada Council for the Arts, which last year invested $153 million to bring the arts to Canadians throughout the country, and the financial support of the Government of Canada. Biblioasis also acknowledges the support of the Ontario Arts Council (OAC), an agency of the Government of Ontario, which last year funded 1,709 individual artists and 1,078 organizations in 204 communities across Ontario, for a total of $52.1 million, and the contribution of the Government of Ontario through the Ontario Book Publishing Tax Credit and the Ontario Media Development Corporation.

PRINTED AND BOUND IN CANADA

To Charla

Our love has been.
I see the rain.
Nothing
is abstract any more.
Denis Johnson, 'Gray Day in Miami'

1

The Stars above the Desert

The beautiful house was empty. Kristin watched from the front window as her sister climbed into her snow-spattered car and drove away, shuttling from one set of worries—Kristin—to another—the noisy, complicated, enviably involving struggles of her family life.

Suzanne had left behind a liveliness in the air through which she had moved and talked. Kristin walked back to the kitchen where there were syrupy breakfast plates to clear. She transferred them to the small dishwasher and sucked her sweetened thumbs. *Diversify*, Suzanne had said. *Find some other activities and interests.* She used a clear, careful voice with Kristin at the moment, stripped of challenge and controversy. In Kristin's mind Suzanne's broad, freckled face still hovered, neutral and patient, ready for her reaction. *I understand you not getting a job for a while if you don't have to. You're in a great situation, when you think about it. Perfect fresh start time. Craig thinks ...* Kristin didn't care what Craig thought. Craig was entirely unsympathetic. Craig was most of the problems Suzanne was now shuttling towards in her rattling Kia on the road back to Pottstown. Craig thought that Kristin had got it made: married to her boss, divorced by her boss and now entitled *by law* to the lifestyle to which she had become accustomed. *You won the Rollover*, he liked to say straight to her face and smiling, as though she wouldn't hear the dirty joke he was pretending he hadn't made. Craig was the sort of dumb and nasty that thinks it's smart. Often, when Suzanne's back was turned, he looked at Kristin, just looked at her for as long as he felt like it, smoking and thinking things.

Kristin was upstairs now, deciding whether she needed to change the sheets of the bed where Suzanne had slept. Kristin lowered her nose to the creased fabric and thought not, catching only a sharpness of lavender. She removed a long curving hair from the pillow and tugged everything straight. Kristin had painted the upper rooms of the house in colours she had seen on *The Grange*, a British TV program that had in the most extraordinary way become a very important part of her life. In the show, the walls of the rooms where the wealthy family lived were painted in rich and sombre colours she didn't like but the servants' rooms downstairs had lovely colours that she spent many hours with swatch books seeking to match. Blues and greens that were spacious and honest, that had a dignity and sadness that were ideal as the containers of her new, ruined life. Not that Kristin spent much time in the upper rooms. The bedding in this one was white, voluminous, heavy, and made soft crunching sounds as she rearranged it. All neat again. A border of broderie anglaise, an intricate pattern of holes, ran across the top of the comforter.

Kristin had with great care and attention to detail redecorated her marriage away. Everything was now to her taste and signified her ownership of this desirable rowhouse. Removing all traces of Ron had been a relief but changing her stepsons' rooms was painful. They had only been there for the odd weekends that Ron had them but Kristin had always loved that rushing influx of youth and energy, even if, except for the youngest, Lionel, they had not liked her back. Beautiful little Lion. The older boys would glare or speak in grudging single words while staring at their devices, but Lion recognized her kindness, her eagerness, and needed it, coming slowly closer and closer. Now she had removed the clutter and colourful walls of childhood and replaced them with tasteful, impeccable adulthood. Sometimes she regretted it.

Kristin decided to go to yoga. That was another activity and interest. Suzanne didn't even know. Kristin went to the room with her wardrobe and changed from pyjamas into the soft second skin of her exercise clothes. Over them, she put on her long quilted coat and collected her mat and bag.

When she went to the front door, she found mail lying there, one piece, for Ron: a catalogue for a clothing company that he had never got round to cancelling. Kristin knew it well, mature men in outdoor wear posing in landscapes, fishing, striding, drinking out of enamel mugs with their shirtsleeves rolled. It would go straight into the trash. She was not his PA any more. It was maddening that she still had to deal with these things. Kristin pulled at it to tear it in half but it was too thick. The pages just twisted in her hands. The whole Ron situation had begun with tasks performed for him, note taking and letter writing and appointments in his diary and travel bookings and gifts for his wife and children. When he formed his own company, she went with him. Those morning drives away from traffic out of Philly into greenness and landscape and his big house near Valley Forge, the crackling sweep of his gravel driveway, that long wrong turning in her life. He was still there, with a new wife now, his third. And Kristin was alone. Almost alone.

Kristin liked walking along with the rolled mat poking out of her tote bag. The spiral of foam was a recognized thing. People knew what it was and saw her walking brightly along, supple and sensitive and responsible. The walk was twenty minutes of mostly straight, harsh road but she liked to do it. Almost no one walked but she did. Kristin was in tune with a different time, historical and civil, walking in the salted channels between crusts of snow with the quick chirping British voices of *The Grange* talking in her head. Kristin admired good penmanship too and handwrote her letters to Henry Banks in navy ink. She tried to make them so beautiful and neat that they looked like you could put the pages upright on a stand and play them on a piano. She put on her hat and gloves and went out.

Henry. Henry was everywhere and nowhere, shaping everything. He was the key signature in which the music of her life was played.

The cold air was rough and quick, the light under grey clouds a thickened white. Unseasonable weather. They were barely into fall and this snow had come suddenly swinging down from the north, flinging whiteness. Kristin liked it, the thrill of this unexpected change. She walked with poise and purpose, her yoga mat protruding from her bag.

Behind the front desk at the yoga centre, the girl's familiar face looked strongly exposed, floating in front of the cabinet of t-shirts and water bottles, smiling Buddhas and detoxing teas, as though it had been cropped out of a different photograph. "Wow," Kristin said. "I like the hair."

"Oh, thank you," said the girl, lengthening her neck with a slight inclination of her head as though the hairdresser were still circling her with a mirror to show her all the angles.

"Dramatic," Kristin said and the girl looked directly at her. "It's great," Kristin repeated.

"I thought, you know, this could work for me."

"Oh, it works. Maybe I should take the plunge instead of." Kristin took hold of her braided ponytail and lifted it up to the side, demonstrating its weary familiarity. "You have to invite change, don't you? Step into the new. Where did you get yours done?"

The receptionist hesitated. "Where did I get it cut?" she asked.

"Yes," Kristin read her name tag, "Layla. Where did you go?"

"Well."

"It's okay. You don't have to tell me."

"No, no. I was."

"It's fine. I understand. We can't all have it done. I probably don't want it anyway."

"It was at Salon Masaya, on Frankford Ave. You have such beautiful thick hair is all. And along with those bangs, so cute."

"I know. I'm a lucky person," Kristin said. "In a lot of ways."

Kristin pushed through the double doors, splitting the lotus flower logo painted on them, and left Layla behind as the doors swung back together. Now, having entered the sanctuary, from small speakers overhead came the sound of flowing water, encouraging a peace of mind that had not been achieved by the small dog shifting from foot to foot outside the main practice room. Laurie was taking the class. Kristin didn't think that Laurie should bring her pug with her, though everyone fussed over it and knew its name, Jasmine. The pug was adorable but unfairly so, because of its indignities, its crushed bulging features, wet and black, its short scraping breaths and urgent, inept waddle. Kristin scratched its furrowed scalp and pulled a velvet ear through her fingers before she went in. Hard to know if Jasmine even noticed. It reacted only to the opening door and shuttled forwards. Kristin kept it back with a raised foot and shut the door.

"Poor thing wants her mommy."

Kristin turned to see the man who'd made this comment, tall and soft in the middle, a dark bulb of hair, smiling. Around him, four women were readying themselves in different areas of the room.

"But if I let her in," Laurie said, "she'd be licking at your faces and blowing her breath over you and you wouldn't want that."

"No, probably not."

Laurie stood on large livid feet, shaking her long fingers loose. Her flesh had been subdued with years of practice. Her belly lay meek and flat behind jutting hip-bones. Hair scraped back, skin clear as rainwater, she smiled generally into the room, a kind of facial hold music, while Kristin deposited her bag and coat and unrolled her mat in a space between the others.

"Okay, okay, yogis," Laurie said. "Somehow it's wintertime already but there is still a sun behind those clouds to salute, so." She stretched up and poured herself down into the first asana. The others followed, growing upwards, folding in half.

Kristin stretched and breathed through the hour, seeing the room in different perspectives, the wrinkled cloth at her knees, her red and white fingers on her mat. Periodically, Jasmine scratched at the door. Kristin looked through the hoop of herself and saw the others in similar knots and star shapes. She felt vibrant with exertion, her heart beating heavily, sweat in her hair. Henry, the things I do for you.

Afterwards, they lay in corpse pose and the lights and shabby ceiling tiles drifted like clouds overhead. Kristin liked lying in corpse pose, at the bottom of things, her bones resting on the floor, like she'd sunk to the bottom of the ocean, discarded. Dying and dying and dying. The relief of a final state.

As she sometimes did, Laurie decided to share an inspirational thought to close the class. "It is suddenly cold and dark," she said, her voice deeper and slower after the hour's yoga. "It feels like the end of the year, like we're all about to hibernate. But you ask a naturopath, or a farmer, or anyone who really understands natural cycles, and they'll tell you this is the beginning. The seeds are falling into the earth and will start germinating now, under the snow, underground. New futures are growing, new possibilities. So while you lie there at rest at the end of our cycle of activity, think of yourself as a germinating seed about to get up and walk into your future."

Oh, it was wonderful how if you were open the world told you what you needed to hear which was what you already knew. Kristin was alive with her very particular future. Suzanne had no need to worry. It would happen. The connection was made. Kristin had been reborn before, when she had met her twin soul, Henry Banks, by chance, on her way down to the Virgin Islands for a vacation. She remembered so well the strange dazzling period of realization that the whole world had changed, down in the blue Caribbean. There was that butterfly that flew into her room and stayed there for several days, its unbelievable colours dancing and gliding. When it settled on her bedspread or curtains she could see the crystalline pattern of its wings, bars of glowing green, dots of yellow, its round, alien eyes and sensitive antennae. You can see the whole universe in a butterfly if you really look, its intricate, perfect machine. It was a sign. That was obvious. It bounced up. It sailed in curves. The butterfly had come to tell her that everything was going to be all right.

After Laurie rang the bell that marked the end of the session, Kristin was the first to leave, her warmth sealed inside her coat. She allowed Jasmine to scuttle in with great relief through the opened door.

During the class more snow had fallen. Kristin walked quickly home into a fresh, speeding wind. Cars thrashed wetly past. On the corner at a cross street the wind whisked up the surface snow and spun it in a little tornado and stopped and did it again. The wind must always spin like that, Kristin suddenly understood, only now it was visible. The snow illustrated the wind and Kristin, noticing, had a little bit more of the secrets of the world revealed to her, things you can't see but are as true as true. The world is a magical place.

At home, she showered and washed her hair. On the edge of her bed, she bowed into the blast of the hair-dryer. From the kitchen, she collected some crackers and baby carrots and dip and took them down to the den. The den was the part of the house where she was most comfortable, warm and half-underground, the snow blue against the glass of the windows. The rest of the house, perfected and separate, hovered overhead. She turned on the TV. If she didn't turn on the TV the silence could accumulate. Amazing how the silence could gather and get louder and louder and seem almost to be about to explode, like a faulty boiler shaking its pipes. It could give her pressure headaches. The TV kept it at bay. She settled on the sofa. Her hair was fragrant and light and voluminous. Before she started the TVO of *The Grange* she had her alerts to check on her iPad. Nothing new had come up for Henry's name on Google. She checked Twitter for mentions. Something in a language she didn't understand which when translated was just about the show going out that night in their country. In a way, it was a relief to search around and find nothing. The searching was stressful, unpredictable, thrilling sometimes, making her heart jolt with a new photograph or a new lie about his personal life. And there were so many people with stupid opinions, people who had never even met him who thought they knew something about him. Less of this now that the final season of *The Grange* had been aired with a frightening flurry of coverage. Sometimes she wished the whole online world didn't exist to confuse her connection with Henry. Once it had all been so simple. He'd held her hand. One day he would again.

She set the iPad down, next to Spiderman. Spiderman lay on the sofa beside her, small and plastic, his stiff arms and legs raised as if for action, holding a stomach crunch position. Lion, little Lionel who loved her, had given her Spiderman one day without telling her. And Spiderman had become a crucial part of the story. It all added up. Kristin picked up the remote and flipped on an old episode. When Henry appeared, she thought she would tell him about the wind and the snow and about what Laurie had said about seeds in winter in her next letter. She would start on it later. Letters flew past all that electronic noise and went right to his hands. Henry's movements on the screen, his expressions, the exhilarating moments of his smiles, his emotions, the dialogue in that beautiful accent that she could speak along with—it was all a timeless connection. She ate and she watched all the precise little moments, her mind fully fastened to them. She could stay like this until the daylight darkened and the neighbours' cars, returning from work, passed like airplanes overhead.

*

The hunger was beginning to hurt. Three days of grinding emptiness, of heat and sudden flutterings in the left side of his body. The relief of small meals in the evenings, monkish bowls of rice and green vegetables that he perceived so sharply, his senses attuned to the rising steam, the warmth and aroma. And afterwards the velvety sensation of being fed that allowed him to fall asleep. In the morning he was hungry again. It was working. It was worth doing. He was becoming what he needed to be, to convince García who, finally, was in London to see him. But it would be a mistake to fast today. He needed energy. He went to his kitchen and ate a banana and two large handfuls of nuts, enough food to relax and feel well but not enough to dull his sharpness. He ate and hummed to himself.

He dressed. He ran his hands down the smoothness of his abdomen. His body was tight. His trousers hung from his hipbones. He chose a khaki linen shirt with button-down pockets that he thought had the right sort of feel: serious, adaptable, with connotations of the military and the desert. Henry checked how he looked in the mirror.

Henry's face was something everybody had to deal with, to assimilate and get over, even Henry. When Henry caught sight of his face he often felt as though he were arriving late at something already happening. His face looked so finished and authoritative. He had the approved lines, the symmetry; he looked how a man should look. His handsomeness could be a shock, as much for him as for others who sometimes also had to process their recognition of him, their sensation of an untethered and inexplicable intimacy. Occasionally Henry thought that it would be nice, warm and relaxed and human, to be a little ugly, to have a face that showed personality in pouches under the eyes' or a large, soft mouth, the face of a character actor, expressing suffering and humour. His own good looks were bland, Henry thought, mainstream, televisual. Hunger seemed to be improving it, its calm masculinity now fretted with sharpness and shadows. Henry had observed long ago that cinematic faces were not normally attractive, not attractive in a normal way. They did not belong on Sunday evening television or in clothing catalogues or any realm of the conventional ideals. The truly cinematic actors, that is. Look at Joaquin Phoenix with his dark stare and scarred mouth or Meryl Streep's long thin nose and subtle, not quite sensual mouth, her large and frightening eyes, her affronting vulnerability. All of them, when you thought about it: Christopher Walken, Jack Nicholson. Bogart and Hoffman and Day-Lewis. Of course the actresses tended to be more straightforwardly beautiful but then overwhelmingly so. Think of the wide landscape of Julia Roberts's smile, an American landscape, honest, expansive, full of hope. No, up until now, Henry's face had been of the reassuring kind that made for success on TV. It had lacked the strangeness and astringency that made for cinema. But now, perhaps, it was coming, with age, with hunger. He observed himself in the mirror. He said, "Ba-ba-ba-ba-ba-ba. Pa-pa-pa-pa-pa-pa. Red lorry. Yellow lorry. Red lorry. Yellow lorry. How are you today? I'm fine, sir. How are you today?"

He checked his phone to see if his taxi had arrived. It hadn't. He stepped out onto his balcony to smoke a cigarette, cupping the lighter flame from the blustery river air. A whirring sound: straight and fast, a cormorant flew low over the water. He should be looking at his pages again. He threw the cigarette away and went in.

He picked up the pages and glanced at them, reminding himself. He bounced up and down on the balls of his feet, swinging his arms. "Ba-ba-ba-ba-ba," he said. "Pa-pa-pa-pa-pa. You can't just walk in here whenever you like. You just can't."

His phone chimed. The taxi was outside. According to the text, Omar was driving. Henry had booked a taxi because he wanted safety between his flat and Soho, a protected preparatory calm. The bike ride was too long, too raw, too sweaty, and he almost never used public transport now. You never knew what might happen. He put the pages in his satchel. He paused in the centre of the room to practise a facial expression, the animation of a friendly and relaxed greeting.

He dropped the expression from his face. He bounced again on his feet then walked on. Locking the front door behind him, he immediately missed the safety of his flat. It would be there to receive him again, to hide him, after whatever it was that happened later in the day.

On the shelf by the exit door he had post. Two letters. He put them into his satchel and stepped outside.

The taxi was a large black people carrier with tinted windows. Inside, he said to the neck in front of him, to the bejewelled hand on the gear stick, "Hi, Omar. You know where we're going?"

"Got the address here. Greek Street."

"That's the one."

Not wishing to talk anymore, Henry pushed his headphones into his ears and put on his pre-meeting music. Years ago at university, as a music scholar, a member of his college choir, he had sung Renaissance polyphony. A sense of competence and self-confidence suffused him when he heard it now. The plainchant of the opening statement, low and horizontal, was followed by the higher voices joining one after the other, merging, ascending, passing one another, opening a great fan of sound. Calm and ethereal, a translucent grid laid over his view of Docklands, of Limehouse and east London passing outside his window. He hummed along with Palestrina's tenor line. In the comfortable hollow of his leather seat, he watched the people outside, the Muslims with waistcoats and hennaed beards, the young mothers, the hipsters of Whitechapel over time giving way to the suited office types of Gray's Inn and Holborn: London's surplus of faces, of human versions, every permutation, all preoccupied, unconscious, milling towards something. At traffic lights the taxi slowed for him to observe a man on a corner holding a phone to his ear and eating an apple, delicately picking with his teeth at the remaining edible flesh by the core. A cyclist shuttled past his window. All these people, blind to his presence behind darkened glass. They would be interested in him, most of them. Their expressions would change. The taxi progressed in halts and short surges into Soho. Henry checked his watch. Good, he wasn't too early. He plucked the flowing harmonies from his ears, paid Omar and stepped briefly into the movement of the street. Keeping his head low, hunched forwards, he walked to a discreet glass door with gold lettering and pressed the buzzer. There was no voice but the door buzzed. Henry pushed it open. He was met by a young man of the assistant type descending the stairs, what Henry's friend Lucas had once referred to as "one of those little shits with the hair." On his t-shirt, much more striking than his actual face, was a very realistic drawing of a gorilla wearing large headphones. He had a pen in his mouth which he removed to say, "Hi, it's Henry, isn't it?" as if he didn't know. "Come on up," as if he owned the place. The guy put the pen back in his mouth and headed up the stairs. Henry followed. At the top, Henry was met by Sally, the casting director, a quiet, tightly organized woman, a great encyclopedist of talent, and one of the most important people in the business. Often it was those people who seemed the least artistic, like they could work happily in any other business. They spoke in the universal language of professionalism, not one that Henry had been obliged particularly to learn. Sally Lindholm could just as easily have run a government department.

"Henry, how nice to see you. Thank you for coming in. How are you?"

Thank you for coming in. The pretense that this was an equal relationship was something that Henry was used to ignoring. The answer to the question how are you was always to be kept brief. Genuine as her friendliness may be, Henry knew not to talk with any unnecessary personal detail. The space accorded for his response was like a box on a form to be filled out. It could only contain so much. "I'm good, I'm good," he answered.

"You're looking well," Sally said. Her friendliness was real enough. It was other people's—actors'—responses to her that couldn't be trusted. They were always straining, eager, beaming, and Sally was like royalty, accepting this as normal, possibly at this point unable to tell the difference between the acting and the real thing, or not caring. "We're ready to go, I think," she said.

"Oh, really? No waiting area? No fellow actors I have to pretend I'm happy to see?"

She laughed. "Not today. You're spared. Shall we go in?"

"Sure. I'm excited to meet the man himself."

"Of course. Do you need anything? Water?"

"Just some water would be great."

"Okay. Seb, could you bring some water for Henry?"

The assistant swept the upper mass of his hair from one side of his head to the other. "I'm on it," he said.

Henry animated his face with warm greeting as he entered the room but he had to wait. García was watching some footage on a laptop. A large man, his folded arms rested on his gut. Sitting low in his chair, his face was sunk down into his beard. He held up one hand to stay Henry and Sally, then decisively slapped the space bar.

"Okay, okay," he said. "Please." He gestured at the seat in the middle of the room facing a camera. "You are Henry."

"I am."

"So, I've seen your work. I've seen you on tape. All very nice."

Henry dropped his satchel by the door and sat down, leaning forward towards García, his forearms on his knees. "And I've seen yours, of course. *Sueños Locos. The Path to Destruction. The Violet Hour. Bricks.* I mean, those are … They mean a lot to me, those films. It's an honour to meet you."

"Okay, okay," García exhaled through wide nostrils and shunted his glasses back up his nose.

Seb swooped down at Henry's feet then backed away. Henry glanced down and saw a bottle of mineral water. Seb settled himself in a seat beside the camera. García said, "So, Mike. You like this character?"

"I don't know about 'like.' I think I understand him. I feel him."

"You think you are like him?"

"Sure. I know where he's coming from, that commitment, that anger. We all are to some extent. That's the genius of it."

García didn't smile or respond. He hit the centre of his glasses again. "So we will read a little bit."

Sally said, "You've got the pages, haven't you?"

"Yep." Henry raised an arm to indicate his bag. "But I shouldn't need them. I'm off book."

"Excellent. Seb, ready to go?"

"Just one …" He pressed a couple of buttons. A small staring red light appeared on the camera. He gave a thumbs-up.

Henry dropped his head down onto his chest, disconnecting, becoming the other thing. He lifted his face. It was tighter, slightly stricken, his gaze significant.

"Julia?" he said.

García, an unlikely Julia, gruff and heavily accented, said, "Hey, Mike."

"Julia, you can't just walk in here like this."

"The door was open."

"What does that mean? You walk through every open door you see?"

"Jesus, Mike. I was just passing and I came in to see."

"You can't do that, Julia. You can't. You can't. I'm just getting things, you know, clear here."

"Okay," García interrupted. "Leave it there."

"Sure." Henry drained back into himself. Uncomfortable, he reached down for the water bottle and twisted the top but didn't yet drink.

"That first 'Julia,'" García said. "It can be softer."

"Okay."

"And you know he is saying the opposite of what he wants. He isn't sleeping. He isn't eating. The war is in his head all the time. He knows he's in trouble. He wants Julia to come in. You have to say, 'You can't just walk in.' Underneath it's, 'You have to come in. Please.'"

"That's what I thought."

"And 'What does that mean?' That line, he's thinking about meaning, he's thinking in a different way, very fast, very conceptual."

"He's like on a whole other level. He's like, yes, but what does that mean? She walks through every open door she sees? It's a description of her, of her freedom. It's, like, the total contrast to him."

"Exactly, exactly. Also, a bit angry. 'What does that *mean*?' It's too much for him. We do again."

Henry sighed and shook his shoulders, looking down then up. "Julia," he said.

"Hey, Mike."

"Julia, you can't just walk in here like this."

"The door was open."

"What does that mean? You walk through every open door you see?"

"Jesus, Mike. I was just passing and I came in to see."

"You can't do that, Julia. You can't. You can't. I'm just getting things, you know, clear here. I'm getting set. I'm making improvements. It's delicate. People need their privacy."

"Okay, that's good."

"Really? You don't want to get more of the scene?"

"No. Enough words. I want to see Mike alone in his apartment."

"Okay, sure." Henry took a drink. The bottle was full to the brim. Water toppled into his mouth. He swallowed. "Sure," he said. "Just ..."

"Just be alone in the apartment."

"Sure. Cool." He closed his eyes and willed himself there. The apartment, as far as he was concerned, had yellowing wallpaper. There was a fridge, old, large, American, with rounded edges. Windows down onto the street. He stood up and paced, quickly, as though his body was a racing thought. He did that for a while then stopped still as though halted by some new idea. He sat down in the chair and stared into the distance, one hand picking at the fabric of his trousers. After a while he swigged from his water bottle with an overhand grip that made it beer. García said, "Okay, okay. Enough."

Henry groaned and rubbed his face with his hands. He felt a drop of sweat, cold, appear at his waist on the right-hand side, rolling down from his armpit.

"You can do it again," García said. "But you have to stop acting like somebody who is acting."

"You mean …"

"Stop acting. Forget us. You're alone in private."

"Okay. Sure." He stared past the blurred mass of García. He hardened his facial expression. Disconnected, he wanted to go to sleep. He thought about going with that impulse and letting his eyes close, but it wouldn't be enough. He got up and paced again. He stopped. He sat down and fidgeted.

"Okay, okay. That's good."

"All right."

"Good. That's enough."

"It's enough? You don't want?"

"No, it's good. We have it."

Sally stood up, holding her notebook to her waist. "Great. So."

"Well, like I said," Henry advanced while he had the chance, hand outstretched, "it's an honour. I'm pleased you called me back again."

García did not stand up. He held out a surprisingly soft and heavy hand for Henry to grasp.

"Okay, okay," he said. "Thank you."

"So," Sally said again, smiling by the door.

When they were the other side of that door, desperate to get a sense of what had happened, Henry said, "Wow, that was quick. For a fourth meeting."

"He's like that," Sally said. "Quick and decisive. It's fine. We'll be in touch."

"Okay. Cool. Okay." Henry resisted the urge to grip her shoulders and say, "Just tell me now." He smiled at her and said, "Amazing. That was Miguel García. Okay. Well. I'll see you next time. I guess I can let myself out."

In the street, he wanted to shout and punch something, to free all of the crushed energy inside him. Instead, he walked quickly for a few yards then turned around and walked in the opposite direction with a destination in mind. Don't act like a person acting. Such drama-school-level bullshit. García had a reputation for brilliance, for spontaneity, for breaking down his actors until, defenceless, they gave him what he wanted. But that couldn't come from stuff like that. Henry wouldn't believe it. Henry didn't need manipulation anyway. He was ready to give García whatever he asked for.

Henry hurried off Old Compton Street with its many obstructing pedestrians into Dean Street and through the door of the Groucho Club. He was furiously hungry and the Groucho cheeseburger was what he wanted right now. The garish, pretentious homeliness of the Groucho was also appealing, certainly more than the watchful grey restraint of Soho House. He signed the register and pushed through the inner door.

A bristle of inspection from those at the bar, carefully dissembled. He could feel a few of them recognizing him: that momentarily prolonged glance before looking away. Their non-reaction was an important facet of their self-respect, a self-respect that Henry knew was nonetheless enhanced by his being there. He walked through the bar, past the piano and down the corridor to a table in the back. He opened his satchel, pulled out his phone and the post he'd forgotten he'd picked up and tossed them onto the table. He raised one hand to attract a waiter and picked up his phone with the other. A waitress appeared, blonde, attractive in her black waistcoat and tie, her long apron, her shining hair tied cleanly back. They hired them for a reason.

"Mr. Banks, what can I get you?"

"Oh. Can I get a cheeseburger and a Diet Coke?"

"Of course. Anything with that?"

"No."

"Great. Sorry, to remind you, if you want to make a call you'll have to take that outside."

"No worries. I know the rules."

He waited for her to go away and put his phone back on the table. He wasn't quite ready to phone Carol, his agent. Instead, he sat back in his seat, tired, molested with afterthoughts, with the image of García waiting for him to leave the room, with the memory of his own performance. That came back to him now in horrifying flashes of clumsy effort that went on who knew how long. Audition room time seems to distend to great length while it is happening and collapse into one catastrophic moment when it is over.

Miguel García was one of the few filmmakers out there that everybody called a genius, a Werner Herzog, a Paul Thomas Anderson, a Scorsese, a man whose interest in you would guarantee the interest of others and who, moreover, made actual works of art. In so doing, he made actors, their faces, their gestures, their names, permanent in the history of the world. He was larger than Henry had imagined, thick-limbed, a slow and stubborn mass. His beard was unpleasant to look at. It was not an outgrowth of lustrous vitality, more a sign of indifference and neglect. His large, square-framed glasses were in the style of no style. They belonged on a man who lived with his mother, who spent hours in public libraries and carried his possessions in plastic carrier bags. That had been García. There was no outward sign of his intelligence, beyond a grumpy decisiveness. Sitting low in his chair, he gave the impression of an animal in an odorous den. He had peered out, judging Henry, deciding whether or not he was worthy of the immortality that he would confer only as a by-product of pursuing the distinctive beauty of his vision. This film, *The Beauty Part*, was preoccupied with the central character, with Mike, with, potentially, Henry. Desire for the part flamed up in Henry, scorched and faded, leaving him even more tired and despondent. Fortunately, his Diet Coke arrived and Henry could take a long pull on its cold caramel flavour, its caffeine and enlivening bubbles. No new messages on his phone, he reached for his post.

The first, larger envelope was an invitation to a short film screening and party that he had no interest in. The second envelope was printed with his agent's company name. That one contained another envelope, decorated with a sticker of a butterfly, in which was a handwritten letter.

It began, *My dearest Henry, it's been so long since we met and yet every day I feel us growing closer together and I know you must do deep down as well. I watch you all the time on The Grange so I can keep seeing your face. I know it so well, I know your expressions, your hair and eyes, the sound of your voice. It is the music of my life.*

Why had this come to him?

What's the latest news I have for you? The strange weather I mentioned in my last letter keeps coming. I had a dream about you last night, back in the airport. And then, down in the islands. Remember how I told you that soon after we met I was down in St. Thomas and I wrote your name in the sand and drew a heart round it? I was there again, looking ....

Henry stopped reading. This letter should not have got to him. Carol's assistant, Vicky, was supposed to screen this stuff out, not just stick it in an envelope and send it to him. This was not helpful right now. This letter did not strike him as endearing or amusing. It was typical of quite a few he'd read in the past. Unsettling, uncanny, full of private madness and incantation and belonging to a live person who was out there right now, thinking about him, who thought she had met him, scrawling his name on pages, on the sand of a beach somewhere, and feeling a compulsion in the world that was about them, about his fate. It was nonsense and harmless, presumably, but so much better not to know, not to have this inside him. It should never have reached him.

The waitress brought his cheeseburger. He folded the letter away and started to eat, terminating the hunger of several days with sweet, granular meat, a pulp of bread, wet tomato, sauces and pickles and handfuls of fries. He ate without pausing. After he'd finished every scrap, every golden fragment of fry, he awoke from the eating, feeling full, stabilized in his centre. He sipped his drink and picked up his phone. A few commercial emails but otherwise nothing. Henry didn't use social media. He went to a newspaper site and read the headlines. In America, a gunman was holding people hostage on a university campus, having killed two already. There were photographs, video footage and live updates. His reading was interrupted when a man walked up and stood beside his table.

"It's Henry Banks, isn't it?"

Henry looked up at a smiling, sly, embarrassed and determined face, a hand held out for him to shake. "Yep. Sorry, do I know you?"

"We did meet once. I'm Steve. I'm a friend of Gemma Lyons who was the AD on *Shooting the Curl*."

"Sure. Gemma."

"There aren't enough Cornish surfing comedies, in my opinion."

"Critics seemed to think there was at least one too many."

"Ha. Well, look, I just wanted to, I know it's kind of against the unwritten rules …"

"Probably don't do it, then."

"All right. But I'm going to anyway. I've got a script. We've got a script …"

"He's doing it. I said don't do it and he's doing it anyway."

"And a production company ready to form."

"That's fine. That's good news. Just go through my agent. I've got to call her now, actually, funnily enough, so if you'll excuse me." Henry gathered his phone, his post and satchel and stood up.

"Sure. I'm sorry. I just. It's perfect for you. I saw you and I had to say something."

"It's fine. Just talk to my agent. And don't do it again." Henry shook the outstretched hand and walked away.

Out in reception, he called Carol.

"It's me, Henry."

"Great. Good. So how was it?"

"Oh, first of all, Vicky sent me some quite unhinged fan mail for some reason. That's really not helping anything."

"Not her. A new girl. Don't worry about it. I'll have her put to sleep. How was Miguel?"

"It was quick. I've got no fricking idea."

"He is hard to read, apparently."

"That's true. I'm telling you that's true. There didn't seem to be anyone else there which maybe is a good sign. If he hasn't got half a dozen in America lined up."

"You never know."

"Do you know if he's seeing other people? You haven't got another client in the mix for this? Tom? Is Tom going up for this?"

"From what I've heard from Sally already, he likes what he's seen of you very much. Of course he'll want a couple of other people on tape."

"Of course."

"Relax, Henry. If it's not this it'll be something else. Plenty of offers coming in for you. This isn't the only line of attack. I still think there could be a slower transition from *The Grange*. You could still do the Hollywood Englishman, rom-com thing. You know I think you'd be great at that."

"But this is the one, though, isn't it? I mean, García. A lead. It's totally Cannes. It's a proper film. It's like a Michael Fassbender role. Has he been offered it, do you know?"

"It would be a great thing to do. Short meeting can be a very good sign. Make your impression. Make your point. Job done. Now do you need any more reassurance or shall we leave it until I've heard something?"

"Sure. I was really just hoping you'd had an immediate call or email, to be honest."

"Soon as I hear anything, I'll call."

"I know you will."

"You're a great actor. You've had a terrific six-year run with a huge TV show. The career move afterwards can be scary but it will all be fine. Lots of interest. Lots of exciting things ahead. Stop worrying."

"I will. Okay. Speak soon."

Henry descended the stairs to the toilet and stood in front of a urinal, hiking his satchel across his back out of the way. A long, relieving piss. He hadn't known he'd needed to go so badly. Amazing how the nerves of an audition annihilated ordinary sensations. He ran calming cold water over his hands and pressed them to his face. He pulled his hands up out of the howling dryer. He walked back up the stairs and looking out through the window in the front door saw, unmistakable, out of place, loose in the world, the large, yellow head of García sailing past. Henry stood for a second and took it in, García's sunlit, sullen, authoritative profile printed on his mind's eye like a face on a coin. What should he do? He wanted to go outside to see more. He turned to the receptionist and said, "Could you put the food on my account?" This felt good, the beginning of an adventure.

The street felt different now, more visual, more cinematic, as though García had summoned it into a stronger existence. There he was, walking down towards Shaftesbury Avenue. Everything focused. The edges of the buildings sharpened, the people and traffic distinct, kinetic. The moment was completed with the scooping flight of a pigeon down from a ledge. Henry decided to follow him, just to observe him and see where he went. From his direction it was obvious that he wasn't returning to the casting suite. Henry paused to maintain his distance and watched which way García turned. Left. Henry hurried on now to avoid losing sight of him.

Nobody noticed García, nobody knew. And why would they? There was no sign to indicate who he was. He had no interest in red-carpet fame. That belonged to his actors. He had better things to be doing. He wore boxy, unfortunate jeans with the sad wrinkled knees of an elephant. His stomach stretched his striped business shirt. He wore a suede jacket. He walked with his head tilted slightly back, looking out through the big square windows of his glasses. García was the centre of the scene and at the same time outside of it, observing and unnoticed. They had turned again now and were walking down Charing Cross Road. Henry saw that a woman had noticed him, Henry, and had taken out her phone to sneak a photo while García walked right past her. She could have reached out and touched him. She had the wrong man. It was Henry who was nothing. He ignored the scratching of her attention, the ugly smirk people sometimes wore when they thought they were getting a picture unseen. When García had moved on, he walked quickly, blindly, past the pivoting woman.

Perhaps García was heading for the second-hand bookshops, maybe the one with art books on the corner, but, no, he continued on. He paused, stopping Henry in his tracks, to look across the street at something, maybe that group of tourists or that glass-fronted Chinese restaurant with large photographs of dumplings in the windows. Something. Something was happening in García's mind, out of Henry's reach, some thought that might become cinema. Whatever it was, it finished. García continued walking.

Henry started to wonder if he shouldn't make use of this opportunity, whether he shouldn't bump into García as if by chance and get him into conversation. Talk about the part. Make an extra push. Successful actors often did this. They campaigned. Henry thought of Kate Winslet phoning James Cameron again and again until he gave her the part in *Titanic*. And all those stories of people showing up to auditions in full costume, writing letters, sending tapes. Naturally, you only heard about the successful ones. There must be many more failures, actors annoying directors, marking themselves out as desperate and unstable, eagerly dousing themselves with the petrol of humiliation and lighting a match. Impossible to calculate. But if he did bump into him, if it had just happened, without Henry having followed him beforehand, then Henry would naturally say hello. It would be strange not to.

García was beyond the shops now, beyond the restaurants and the theatres, heading towards the corner of Trafalgar Square. He waited at traffic lights to cross over at the National Portrait Gallery. Hanging back, Henry saw García's untidy hair brushing the collar of his suede jacket as he looked from side to side. The lights changed and García crossed. Henry waited a moment and crossed himself as the lights were changing back. A car moving towards him braked hard, lurching up on its suspension. Henry ignored it, raising no hand of apology. He watched García among multiplying people turn right into Trafalgar Square, along the low front wall of the National Gallery. Henry followed. To his left, the blatting of an amplified voice, the applause of a crowd gathered around a street performer. García turned through the small gateway and walked slowly up the steps to the gallery's main entrance. So this was the destination, the end to the walk. And Henry hadn't lost García through some private door he couldn't enter. This was an invitation to speak to the man.

Inside the gallery, García stood under the coloured dome with one hand on top of his head. He saw where he wanted to go and pushed through a swing door. Henry did the same, pushing the same smeared brass plate on the heavy door. García was standing at the end of a large red room with paintings glowering down.

Henry turned and faced one of them, to look as though he was looking at paintings. He stood still in the busy institutional hush, the active quiet of people pausing and passing. He felt self-conscious. This was on the verge of going wrong. He would have to act soon if he wasn't going to be spotted first and then García might choose to ignore him and then what? He had to do it or go home. He stared up at a face from the Renaissance, grey, lean, bearded, young.

The man held large iron scissors in one hand and stared down at Henry. He wore a sumptuous silk jacket and large red trousers or pantaloons or whatever you called them. That was why Shakespeare was so rarely done in period dress: the costumes looked ridiculous. Henry, pressed by the man's unshifting gaze, mentally greeted him as though he were really standing there, staring silently out of his varnished century. When Henry looked around again, García was gone.

Henry followed in the direction he must have gone and searched for him among the many incidental people. He wasn't in the next room. He wasn't in a larger room of huge, colourful Italian paintings that Henry vaguely saw as a turbulence of gods and Christs and draperies. Another room, other people, none of them García. This was typical, this was indicative—Henry felt it suddenly, the landslide sensation of failure. He would not find García and he would not get the part. Henry hated thinking this way, interpreting signs, anxiously scrying the future, but helplessness made him as superstitious as anyone else. *I wrote your name in the sand. Driving home, the brightest rainbow I ever saw*. What was meant to be. If fame had taught him anything it was that everybody was mad in that way, in the dark privacy of their thoughts. Fame pulled it out of them like magnets, the weird personal connections, the destinies, the universe wanting things for them, or needing them to go through things first, to help them learn.

García was gone, had disappeared among the visitors from many countries, leaving Henry with only his mad analysis. Henry walked at speed, openly hunting now but without expectation of success. When he did find García, inconspicuous in another of the large rooms, a short stout man looking at a picture, stepping backwards to get a different view, momentum carried Henry straight to him.

"Mr. García," he said.

García turned, confused, like a man woken, and then said, "Ah, it's you."

"It is."

"Miguel. You should call me Miguel. Not Mr. García."

"Miguel. Isn't this funny?"

"Funny?"

"Funny peculiar. To run into you like this in here."

"Oh, sure. A coincidence. Yes."

"Exactly. I sometimes come here after meetings, you know, to refocus, to connect with some art."

"I see."

"And why are you here?"

"Why? Maybe the same reason. Why wouldn't I be here? I'm not in London so often and to see these great works, I mean, come on." With a slight swing of his shoulders, García indicated the paintings all around. "There are great works in just this room, Spanish painters, as it happens, that are worth a ticket to London. Look at this one I'm looking at. Velázquez. The greatest. The life of the court made him a bit crazy, I think, but that happens to all artists dealing with power and money. But that's a different story. Here we are with God. Do you know what this is?"

"It's Christ. After the flagellation, the whipping."

"Yes, and this child?" García shifted to his right, pointing with a stubby finger. "This child is the Christian soul. A child I suppose because the soul is innocent, new in the world. And the angel standing behind is encouraging the soul to contemplate the suffering of Christ, still tied up and bleeding."

García was energetic, released from the judgmental passivity of the audition room. Henry was thrilled to be beside his enthusiasm, to be the recipient of his thoughts. He could listen to García explaining the painting all day. He looked at the picture himself and saw something.

"Oh," he said. "It looks like the child, the soul, is looking at Jesus's face at first but he isn't. The angel is showing him Jesus's back, all torn up and bloody. God. It's weird. Like they're looking at a TV."

"That's an interesting comparison you make."

"I suppose. I just meant the way that they're looking at it."

"Intense, no? Contemplating the wound. I think it is the most beautiful, most terrible thing, this child soul made to look at the torture victim and feel his suffering. My feelings about it are absolutely contradictory. As I think they must be. I grew up with this Catholicism. My feelings are contradictory like they are about any big thing in your life. On one side, the Nietzsche side, I am repulsed. Why obsess with this darkness, this pain? Why always turn your thoughts towards it? And this coercion of the child, I feel it in my childhood. That is very dark, too. Life is also flourishing, health, abundance, joy. Why not face towards that and contemplate it? Why not direct the soul to that? But the other side in my thoughts is that this is true. Life is full of pain and isolation and binding. The way Christ is helpless with his hands tied. No one escapes it. And the sympathy in the image, the gentleness, the solidarity, the reassurance of the angel. It's beautiful. It's what people need, you know. There is this suffering but it makes sense. It is part of a plan."

"It is beautiful." Henry looked at the soft, pained face of Jesus, the modest halo of brighter light around his hair, the delicate spattering of blood on his loincloth and thigh, the child, hands clasped, twisting around to look. "It's a profound thing."

García was smiling at him. "So, you? What do you like to look at here?"

"Oh, that. Well, all of it really. I mean it's all, you know, stunning."

"But if you are going to show me just one thing?"

"Oh, okay. You want me to? I tend to like the more modern things, I suppose you could say. I can show you."

"Please."

"Okay." Henry looked around for an exit in the direction of the Impressionist paintings, sure that he would find something in there. "We go this way." As they set off, he said. "Thank you, by the way, for seeing me earlier. I really think the script is amazing and the part. I can't stop thinking about him. I feel him, you know."

"I understand."

"I mean, I …"

"You don't have to tell me. It's okay. I see it."

"You see it?"

"In your audition. I know you are serious. I know you want it. Where are we going?"

"It's ... oh, it's this way, I'm pretty sure."

As they entered the rooms of pretty Impressionist colours, floral landscapes and beach scenes, thronged by many tourists, Henry worried that he'd made the wrong improvisatory choice. The pictures were too sweet, too enjoyable, and García would think he was simple-minded. There was nothing profound about pain and the human condition here. For this reason, a smaller, starker painting caught his eye.

"Ah, here it is," he said. They approached a depiction of Paris under snow, whites and greys, winter light, an elegant, urban emptiness. "I've always liked this painting. It has a purity to it."

"You don't like people so much. Everything whited out."

"I don't mean that. It has a starkness. It's silent. That winter silence. Maybe I do mean that. And it's modest. It doesn't attract attention to itself so much. It's real."

"Pissarro is always like that. Not theatrical."

"Exactly."

García leaned in to the painting, bringing his face within a few inches. With one hand, he held his throat. His eyes behind the large lenses flickered. The strange intimacy of seeing his naked eyes behind his glasses. He straightened again. "Very nice."

"Oh, it's my pleasure."

"It's very extreme, you, the character of Mike. It's not easy, it won't be easy, to build to that ending."

"I know. I see that."

"And the starvation. He must be very thin, like a spectre."

"Like a ghost. Exactly. It's like he behaves like he dies in Iraq. He's like the ghost of himself, haunting his old life in that apartment."

"That's right. Good, good. There's no courage, you understand, in what he does in the end."

"Because he's already dead."

"So there's no fear." García scratched his forehead with four fingernails, reaching across with his elbow lifted high. "I have to go," he said. "Back to the hotel. I have to go out."

"That's a shame." Henry felt unreasonably jealous, envious of whoever would have García's company later. He wanted to stay with him. Everything was so close to his grasp. He was feeling relaxed with the great man. He said, "You know who you remind me of a bit, I don't know if anyone has said this to you before, is Kubrick."

García shook his head. "People always want the familiar. It's a mistake. One auteur with a beard and glasses is like another. 'This film is $8^1/_2$ meets When Harry Met Sally.' You know. Like this script, I know people will say this film is like Taxi Driver meets something or other. It is not. It is different. It is hard to deal with new things, so people want the same. The only thing that comes out looking the same is people's shit."

"I'm sorry. I didn't mean …"

García laughed. "Oh, no. Not you. I'm not saying you. You just reminded me. I must go."

"Sure. I'll show you out."

"No, no. You stay here with your white Paris."

"Fine. Well, it's been a pleasure. I hope to hear from you soon."

"I know you do. Maybe I can make you happy. Maybe I can't."

"You certainly can. The question is will you."

"That's true. The question is will I." García clapped Henry on the shoulder with a heavy, jolting hand. "See you, Henry."

*

Henry dropped his satchel by the wall and kicked the door shut behind him with his heel. He went to put on some music, to open the balcony doors, to put on the kettle. The flat needed disturbance, energy. The stillness, the banal disarray of his possessions was disheartening. There was an intimation of failure caused simply by being him. He needed change, music, air. The flat was modern, built in the nineties, clean, spare, hard. Beneath the slight messiness, it took no deep impression of his presence. The bare floors, the white edges remained distinct, according to the architect's design. Henry had bought the flat a few years ago, during the second season of *The Grange* when he was already contracted for the third and had real money coming in, a future. He couldn't remember when he'd got the idea that he wanted to live in Docklands but he'd spoken of it to an estate agent and let the rest happen while his attention was mostly elsewhere, during a busy filming schedule. It involved a number of processes, visits, meetings, surveys, signatures, bank transfers, none of which on their own felt like buying a house but at the end of it all he had one.

The flat served its function of separation. He was out of town, down along the widening river, in the new area of the money industries, gleaming towers of stacked offices, small squares with modern sculptures, chain restaurants and fitness centres. The wind rang around empty spaces and the curved iron of benches and railings. The Docklands was unlike the rest of London. Its appearance was anonymous, modular, global, financial. Henry liked this, although at times the inconvenience was annoying—the endless, halting drive up the Commercial Road to get in and out of town. And he was far from everybody else, from his friends in Clapham or Crouch End or Kentish Town. Still, where he was between Canary Wharf and Limehouse, he had the river path and the river, the river smell and wave sounds, the passing boats and the breadth of space looking across the water that could not be found elsewhere in the city. Standing on his balcony, he could relax into a primitive animal alertness, feeling the changing power of the wind, scanning the eastward distances. The place was lavish with light, flashing off the water and glass and metal. Evenings were colourful, buildings fading to sombre bronze then turning inside out with their lit interiors clear through the darkness.

All that brilliant glare was to the left of his balcony. Opposite, on the other side of a small canal, were other flats, each with its own balcony. Gaunt cormorants visited the canal, and large loud gulls. His neighbours worked in the banks and investment companies nearby and were rarely in their flats during the day. They appeared on their balconies sometimes at the weekends, lingering over pastries and fruit with a determined show of leisure. Henry was an anomaly here. He looked at his neighbours and the people in their suits and skirts passing in and out of the tall buildings and thought them tedious and technical, interchangeable, and clearly mad in their commitment to the machine they served that gave them only those weekend breakfasts to enjoy. At times, though, he envied them their busyness, their scheduled hours and overtime, the clear shapes of their lives. Their working days began before Henry was awake, leaving him in sole occupancy of his building. He envied also the apparently direct proportion of effort and reward. His life was so dependent upon a casino of chances. Right now it depended upon the opinion, the smallest subjective whim, of Sally Lindholm and Miguel García.

Today Henry had met Miguel García, one of the great film directors of the age. His neighbours might have heard of him—perhaps as the man who made that film with all the real sex—but they certainly wouldn't recognize him. Henry was alone with this significance and his sense impressions of the man himself, the solidity, the open chest, the tilted angle of his head, his hair sweeping his collar. In his bedroom, Henry stood in García's attitude for a moment, chin up and feet planted, anchored, looking out at the world. Henry saw García's slow, determined walk down Charing Cross Road, he saw his grimace of concentration as he looked at the Pissarro painting. Henry unbuttoned his shirt and took it off. The linen was stained in dark circles under the armpits. Henry sniffed: that sour reek of audition sweat, a distinctive odour of fear and effort. He threw it on his bedroom floor and put on a running top, swapped his trousers for shorts. He wanted to get back outside to release the day's compressions, the balked energy, the compacted anger inside him. He felt as if his whole body wanted to shout. He shut his balcony doors again and drank a mug of water by the kitchen sink. He pushed his earphones back into his ears. This time they were connected to a runner's mp3 player that sat in a special strap around his left bicep. He locked his door and shoved his keys deep into his pocket.

On the Thames Path he joined other runners. There were always other runners here to fall in with, relentless A types taking a break in their money-making day to work on their cardio. They ran in talkative pairs or faster and alone, sweat-streaked, mouths open, eyes flatly processing information, disconnected and suffering. Henry set off on his usual route too quickly, an effect of his agitation, and soon burned through his jittery excess of energy. He arrived back at his building tired and heavy, feeling the bones in his legs quietly aching, jolted by the hard surface. The shower did a good job of removing the day, full force and as hot as he could stand it. Afterwards his skin felt tight and tender and new.

He put on sweatpants and a t-shirt. With wet hair, he sat cross-legged on his sofa and ate a large bowl of cereal while watching TV on his laptop. Texts were coming on his phone. There were places he could go tonight, people to hang out with if he wanted to. But he didn't want that. A call came in while he was eating, the word "Mum" showing on the screen. He couldn't be bothered to deal with her today. He let the phone ring off. A minute later it throbbed with a voicemail that he wouldn't listen to this evening either. He needed to curl into himself, to find comfort and darkness. He watched more TV and smoked a joint that had him sinking into the sofa, limbs full of slow and weighty vibration. He took his laptop with him to bed and watched some porn, a compilation of women giving handjobs. He liked it when he could see their breasts, when they looked directly into the camera and said encouraging and warmly insulting things. He liked it when they smiled. It all produced the familiar convulsion, a satisfaction, and the emptiness that preceded sleep.

*

Henry remade himself in the mornings. Simplicity. Light. Breath. Yoga. A glass of water. A shower. The process was delicate. He wanted to empty himself out, to meditate, to attune to the particular weather, to connect with the innocence of the day before the inner clamour started. Recently, this was becoming more and more difficult. He walked a fine line. Any small excess of feeling, a single anxious thought, could tip him over.

He avoided media. News of a film, trailers for TV shows, interviews with actors could all hurt him with an envy that felt like cramp, like impotent anger at injustice. He knew that it was wrong, that seeing yet another photograph of Benedict Cumberbatch or Tom Hiddleston made no difference to anything, but he was helpless, particularly now when everything hung in the balance. The therapeutic platitudes, there is enough for everybody, rejoice in the success of others, were useless. No, he sealed himself from it all in the mornings. The world of entertainment, for everybody else, for his hard-working neighbours, a pleasure, a diversion, a variety of appealing products, was for him a jagged reality of familiar faces and gossip, of missed opportunities and others' galling triumphs. He knew he shouldn't think like that. Meditate on abundance, on loving-kindness.

A day to get through. Another whole day of not knowing. Hanging in space between one world and another. What could he do? Make useless gestures with his arms? He could flap. There was no availing effort he could expend, any more than if he was waiting for the results of a medical test. Days to endure like this. It debilitates you, the weightlessness, the lack of grip. It wastes the muscles of the will.

He drank green tea, sipping the warmth and mild flavour. Small sensations. Steadiness. Outside, the wind pushed low corrugations over the surface of the canal. Huddled clouds. Gulls striving through the air. The sound of a boat's engine. From somewhere nearby, the beeping of a vehicle reversing. London: always grey, always worried, always working.

Henry went to his piano to play for a while. A new purchase—Henry had had the piano delivered when *The Grange* ended, knowing that there would be hours to fill. An expensive, glossy upright, it had a ringing sound that Henry could punch out in big gusts and feel that release or could make sing softly. A good piano for Mozart, it articulated clearly. On the top was a pile of sheet music. The physical action of sifting through them for something to play was so familiar, and the scores themselves, the antique fonts and black borders and elaborates cartouches, brought back the many hours of childhood practice and reminded him: he had a voicemail from his mother. He might as well get it out of the way now.

He collected his phone from his bedside table and took it to the sofa. He sat down with one leg up on the seat, leaning back against the armrest, a posture of relaxation unconsciously adopted, meant to forestall any agitation. There had been no other messages overnight, nothing from his agent. His mother's voice began quietly, as always. He could see her sitting in the green armchair in front of the wall of bookshelves, his father dimly, annoyingly, present in some other part of the house, or out in the garden, out of earshot. Or perhaps that was him playing on the home piano rather than the radio playing.

"This is a message for Henry." Always this tautologous opening, as though after hearing Henry's recorded voice she thought that someone else might be listening. The uncertainty, the hesitancy, was important, though; it expressed the sense of threat she felt from technology and suggested the unpredictable organization of Henry's life. Who knew who was there and using his phone? "Call me back when you get a chance. I know your father would love to hear from you. You should call him. Okay then. Bye for now."

A short message. They had become shorter in response to Henry's perfunctory responses. At some point he would have to deal with this nonsense about his father's script but Henry still hoped that they would eventually see sense and give up.

Sitting on the sofa, deleting his mother's message, Henry was determined to remake this connection and also felt sure that he could sort out the situation with his parents. Both of these thoughts were forgotten two hours later when Carol rang him to tell him that he'd been cast as the lead in Miguel García's next film.

*

The flat was too small to contain him. He had to go out. He texted Rob, who was in a Pinter in the West End. They met after the show, Rob's eye sockets still reddened by the astringency of makeup remover. He hugged Henry. "Mate," he said. His voice was rough and resonant, his gestures large and flowing, still scaled up to fill an auditorium. He gripped Henry's biceps and looked affectionately into his face. "Been a while. Shall we go and do a thing?"

"Let's do it. Let's ride your perf high."

They started in the yellow and brown light, the wood panels and intricate cut glass of a pub. A couple of the other members of the cast went with them. They drank beers in the private centre of the small stir they made with celebrity and good looks. Years before, Rob and Henry had been in the Royal Shakespeare Company together, a long season in Stratford-upon-Avon of the history plays. In that small town along its pretty river, a place numb with gentility and heritage conservation, devoid of anything to do in the wet darkness of autumn, a darkness that began at five o'clock, they entertained each other, partying hard. The derangement became ritual. They were committed to a particular recipe, vodka and cocaine, which they called, for reasons Henry couldn't remember, dog oil and dog powder. They travelled a long way into each other's madness in those months of raw escapade, blasting histrionic talk at each other in the weak light of dawn. They knew each other like houses they had ransacked. It left them no choice but to love each other. Now they met infrequently but they both knew they could rely on the other to go out and get messed up at a word of instigation. They were soldiers.

At the pub, Henry gave Rob his news.

"You fuck," Rob said. He punched him in the chest. "That's amazing."

"I know," Henry said. "Fucking A."

"Wow," Rob said. "Jesus." He leaned back and scrutinized Henry as though he might be lying, as though struggling to get him in focus. Henry sat still, grinning. "Just wow."

"I know. It's big."

"Why did I just buy you a drink? Your round, surely?"

"I'll buy you two, if you want."

After closing time, they moved to the blue light and ranks of glowing bottles in a bar. After that, Henry suggested Shoreditch House. There they decided to drink single malts and to make toasts in Scottish accents that became Irish accents and Irish toasts after Henry used the phrase "the old country." A girl attached herself to Henry, one of the crowd that had come from the theatre. One of the club members was, strangely enough, from Rob's tiny hometown, now working in online something or other. They talked with animated nostalgia. The girl was pretty and required little attention. She sat next to Henry and they established that they would go home together with the pressure of thighs pressed together and later hands mingled below the tabletop and then one slow, binding look into each other's eyes. From then on they kept their secret and did nothing to endanger the arrangement, barely addressing one another. Rob was good company. Rob had many anecdotes, as everyone did when they were in a show. The whisky made Henry sentimental. Old friends, the old country. He missed them with a drunk's sudden plangent emotion. He went up onto the roof to smoke a cigarette among the other smokers. He exhaled up into the sky. The girl—her name was Nikki—appeared beside him and laid her head on his shoulder.

In the back of the taxi, Nikki played with her fingers on Henry's thigh. She leaned across him as if to look at something through his window and dropped her hand onto his fly.

Henry thought that people denigrated casual sex unfairly, applying a morality that wasn't generous or sympathetic. He found it moving, the quick transition between strangers to nakedness and fierce close contact. It expressed a plain human need, without words, without personalities even, just iterations of the human types finding relief from their solitude in pleasure. Henry liked Nikki. She did not seem to be responding to his fame the way some women did. She did not feed on him, on the idea of him. You could look at some women and see in their smile and half-closed eyes that they were involved with some unreality happening in their heads, some wrong fulfillment, some point scored in life. She was very focused on their bodies, to the extent that she seemed almost indifferent to him, working on some pure escalation inside herself. To reach the top in the end she had to rear away from him, looking blindly up at the ceiling. Afterwards, she walked to the bathroom on the flats of her feet with no tension or self-consciousness in her body. She sang under her breath. Maybe she was too disconnected. Maybe she was in some kind of psychological state and Henry was part of an episode. Or perhaps she was in a relationship and didn't want to linger or talk. She came back in driftingly, scratching something away at the corner of her mouth. A boat sounded its horn outside and she turned and smiled at Henry. That was one of the nice things about living in this part of town, the noises that boats sometimes made at night, that daub of lonely sound phoning across the darkness, or the faint thud of music and wispy cheering from a party boat. Still gently drunk, lying in the warmth of the sheets, Henry enjoyed it, the wide spaces of water and night it evoked that felt in that moment like a private kingdom, an extension of him.

"It's like Oslo," she said.

"Is it? I always think it's a bit like Hong Kong here."

She walked over to the window, bent apart the slats of the blind. "Sparkly black," she said.

"What?"

She didn't reply. She wandered slowly back from the window, reading the spines of books and DVDs on his shelves before picking up her clothes from the floor.

"It's nice here," she said. "You must have a nice life."

"I must," Henry answered. "I must."

Nikki didn't respond. She had taken her phone from her jeans pocket and sat on the end of the bed, still naked, reading messages in its glaring screen. She did this for a while. Henry could see the concentration in the back of her neck, the exposed ridges of her spine. Maybe a message from her boyfriend. Who could say? She dropped the phone on the bed, pulled on her underwear and socks, clipped herself back into her bra, pulled on her jeans and soon was again a public person, fully dressed in the middle of the night. She said, "I was sorry when you and that actress Hayley Whatsername broke up. You seemed like a nice couple."

"Okay."

She came over to Henry and, bending down, kissed him on the forehead as though he were her sleeping child. Definitely something going on with that girl. When she was gone, Henry was left alone with his images of the night, with his thoughts of the future without her distracting him. He could think of her wandering naked in his room before she'd said that crap about Hayley that was none of her business. Forget that stuff. He was moving towards something bigger and brighter. Another boat sounded as it navigated the river. The thing with cinema that made it different from theatre and TV and made him want it so much was that film was the world. It merged with the world. It was about real light and places, space and atmospheres, and about being a person, not acting them. You couldn't get how Nikki had been in the room on stage, not really. You couldn't be that quiet and alone surrounded by an audience. What Henry wanted was to be someone on screen, not performing someone in the theatre with its vocal projection and the strain of transformation. He could see all that in the coarseness of Rob's behaviour and fatigue. In the theatre you launched your interpretation of a character out at the audience. Actors gave their Hamlet, one after another, gave their Willy Loman and their Blanche Dubois. In the cinema you just were that person in that place. No one "gave" their Travis Bickle. There was only De Niro with his twitchy gestures and shaved head and weird grin. And everyone imitated those, doing their impression of this undeniable, immortal thing. The more a screen actor carried his essence from one part to the next the better it was. The film actor is cast (Miguel García had cast Henry) to be, not to play. You make the smallest gestures. You stand still. You mumble and throw away lines. In *The Grange*, Henry had felt theatrical, hitting his marks and propelling the plot. Sunday night television was what repertory theatre used to be. They wore expensive costumes, were clear in their emotions and impersonated the past. Now he would have his chance to make a real movie, to be the star that you stare at, fixed above you, barely acting at all. And what comes out of that radiance, a thousand splintering rays of magazine covers and interviews and product campaigns and fans quoting dialogue and internet parodies and academic analysis and midnight screenings, all that would be beyond his control. He would be at the centre of it only, a permeating light.

*

His mother picked up on the sixth ring so Henry was already relaxed with the prospect of leaving a message on the machine when her live voice startled him.

"Hey, Mum. It's me."

"Hen, how are you?" She called to his father. "It's Henry." In recent years a phone call in that house had become an event that needed immediate explanation.

"I'm pretty good. I got the part."

"What part?"

"The part. The lead in the next Miguel García film. It's called *The Beauty Part*."

"Is he the Mexican director who designs things?"

"Designs things?"

"Does drawing?"

"No. He's Spanish. He made *The Violet Hour* and *Sueños Locos*."

"Well, you're obviously very pleased. Good for you. What luck."

There it was. It hadn't taken long. Luck was the word she always used, as though talent, effort or deserving had nothing to do with it. Henry was always just lucky in precisely the same helpless way that she was unlucky, having her children when she did and ending a singing career that had barely begun. There was no arguing with her. Instead, he simply reused the word with emphasis in the hope that she might hear it.

"Yes, amazing luck."

There was silence for a moment while she thought of something else to say, a silence Henry refused to fill.

"When does it start filming?"

"Not for a while. Dates aren't actually set yet. Which is good. I've actually got to lose quite a lot of weight."

"Oh, no. Do you?"

"Yes, I do."

"How much?"

"A lot."

"But why?"

"For the part, obviously. García sent this amazing email about his vision for the film which is really all about my character, Mike. He's back from Iraq and, you know, traumatized, and he ends up taking care of this single mother and her daughter and he decides to take out this dangerous loan shark she owes money to. It's very processy, very quiet, lots of preparation, like *The Day of the Jackal* kind of thing half the time. Anyway, García's idea—I don't know why I'm telling you all this—is that he's a cracked version of the American hero ideal, which is obviously much closer to reality than the ideal. The thinness is about intensity and separation. It's a psychological image. García says he wants to X-ray part of the American brain."

"If it's about America shouldn't he be very fat?"

"That's a good point, Mum. I'll definitely pass that on. Fat, thin, two sides of the same thing. And fat would be easier to achieve, probably."

"I'll get your dad. You can tell him about it. He will ask you about *The Runaways*, just so you know."

"No doubt he will. Put him on."

Henry heard the knock of the phone being set down on the table and his mother saying, "He's got that part," and then, exploiting her opportunity to be exasperated despite not knowing herself five minutes ago, "You know what part. With the famous Spanish director."

He heard the phone being picked up again. "How's my famous son?"

"I'm great. I've got the lead in the next Miguel García film."

"Sounds tremendous."

"It is. It's huge. All the big festivals. It's the big next move."

"Well, don't fuck it up."

"That is the plan. Not to."

"So you're going to be pretty busy, I expect."

"I am. I will when it gets going."

"I know you said your agent wasn't the right person to show *The Runaways*."

"Dad, I don't know who is. She certainly isn't. She's an actors' agent. She doesn't handle scripts, let alone musical theatre scripts."

"Yes, but there must be other people in that agency. I went online and had a look and there's this person Simon Field or Simon Feld, something like that. He has playwrights that he looks after."

"You should send it to him, then. You never know. You might be lucky. Oh, Dad, my agent is actually calling me at this very moment. My phone's flashing. I better go."

★

The strange thing was that Henry could not feel his own fame, could not see himself out in the world, while he could see other people's very clearly, the interviews, the awards, the adverts, the images. He could see them all the time. The success of other people was solid and undeniable and always increasing. But his gaze burned through his own photographs and press appearances, annihilating them. They counted less, precisely because they were him. Even people stopping him in the street, asking to take selfies with him, could not convince him. It was transitory, silly, and left no trace inside him.

Nevertheless, he was famous. Six years of a TV show that millions watched and that had gone around the world meant that people knew who he was, even if only indistinctly. His voice was already inside their minds. They had imbibed him. He was installed as something familiar and safe. This gave him traction on their attention, potentially on the big decisions they made in their lives. This made him money for very little effort. He sat in a booth with headphones on and said to them, "Does your bank treat you like a real person?"

*

In the gym, Henry gripped the handles of the cross-trainer and pulled and pushed and shuttled the foot-plates back and forth. He worked through the first prickling sensation of fullness under the skin and broke a sweat, moving then loosely, rhythmically. He listened to his own music through his earphones and glanced up from the changing numbers on the machine to the music videos playing overhead, R&B tracks, the female shapes of the dancers, the exaggerated globes and narrow triangles emphasized in slow bends and swooping close-ups. Impossible not to look, designed to light up his hindbrain. Losing weight was simple, a question of basic maths. Less energy in, more energy out. The flesh will burn to keep you alive. He used the cross-trainer for an hour and stepped off, his legs trembling on the disquieting stability of the static ground. He went to use the weights.

To be Mike he needed muscles that were worked, knotted, a kind of weathered-in strength made in the world of combat and afterwards, anxious in his apartment, getting smaller and fiercer. García had sent him many images of American soldiers in Iraq and Afghanistan and many had the swollen bulk of prison yard bodybuilders, top-heavy chunks of American force. García was clear that he shouldn't look like that, inflated with defensive swagger. He should be broken down and resistant, realist and dangerous. García had sent him photographs of thorn trees bent by the wind to show him what he meant. García told him to think about the physical world of the combat zone, prefabricated structures, dust and sand, weapons and vehicles, hardness and emptiness and temporary and how you carry that sense of a purely practical and collapsible world with you back into your life.

Henry slipped in his sweat on the leather seat. He got up and towelled it away. He sat down again and sipped water. His fingers were stiff, handling the bottle awkwardly. His arm shook. A woman walked past, groomed for exercise, her hair under a broad black headband. She smiled at Henry. Henry sat back and put his hands on the handles and hoisted the stack of weights up behind him.

García had told him to think about camaraderie among soldiers, the dependency that led to deep love. He sent him photographs of sleeping soldiers. Boyish and vulnerable they rested, helpless in dreams and exhaustion. Henry was supposed to look at them and feel tenderness and to think about all that Mike had lost.

*

Henry opened a tin of tuna and pressed the severed lid down on the fish and poured away the cloudy brine. He levered out the lid with his fork and took the tin over to his balcony to eat. Flakes and spiralled chunks that were smooth in his mouth. Flavour of salt and metal and flesh. Afterwards, he ate a green apple. He cut it into sections and ate it piece by piece, its spurts of sour juice seeming to accelerate his digestion. Hunger made his meals slow and sacramental. It made them strange. He observed the transformation involved in absorbing these external objects into himself, a tin of tuna and an apple becoming his own body, breaking down in chemical darkness, filtering into his cells. The weight was coming off fast. After little more than a week, his trousers hung from the gaunt knobs of his hipbones. The mirror showed his face tired and hollowed, a face of religious suffering. The hunger should be like that, a purification, a preparation for being Mike. That was the best way it could be. He would go out less. He needed to get to a low weight and hover there, waiting for the shooting to begin.

*

Once a day he went to the gym and watched the numbers and the writhing women on the screens. He passed the other hours in his flat. He watched the lights in the other flats come on in the evening, the lights across the water. Sparkly black.

Daily refusals. Drinks. A play's opening night. A charity gala. The opening of a menswear store. An interview with a Spanish magazine and an American podcast. A panel show on the BBC. Turning them all away made him feel stronger and more certain. And it made them want him more. He could feel it.

The problem with hunger was the tiredness. Eating allowed you to rest for a little while but hunger meant an unquiet, anxious body. In the morning he tried to play the piano and found his fingers inaccurate, slow to arrive at the next key. He stumbled, making a garbled, amateur noise, and gave up. He went and lay down on the sofa.

On the other side of the room, the piano still shone, pristine. In childhood, the baby grand stood on its fading rug (it still did), and loomed over him with a kind of disappointed authority, as though it waited for someone who could, finally, live up to it. Henry's mother played it sometimes with a wistfulness and sensitivity meant to attract attention. When it did and Henry or his brother or father said something, she reacted as if some fragile privacy had been violated. She would break off and go to some other part of the house, her point about her talent and her wasted life eloquently made. At the church hall recitals she sometimes gave with Henry's father on the piano, singing Schubert and Schumann and whatever, she would receive the applause at the end and the compliments over the tea and sherry afterwards as proof against her husband and sons, victory in an argument that Henry and Julian had never, in fact, joined. Henry's father played the baby grand with a kind of boisterous self-regard, making the great composers live again. At that same piano, he wrote his own music, the elaborate sonatas and the ponderous Victorian-style songs for *The Runaways*, his musical about the elopement of Elizabeth Barrett and Robert Browning that he was convinced Henry could get on to the West End stage for him. Henry should never have given him any advice at all. The title had been changed from *September 12th*, the day of the elopement, after Henry had pointed out that everyone would assume it would be about the day after September 11. With either title, this was not what London's theatres were crying out for, something where the male lead had huge lamb-chop whiskers and sat down every five minutes to write a poem about love or Rome or the Pope, which he then stood up and sang. The whole thing reminded Henry somehow of a Christmas cake, the unpleasant richness of dried fruit and glacé cherries and alcohol and icing, traditional, festive, indigestible.

Henry picked up the TV remote and held it on his chest but didn't switch the TV on yet. Over that preposterous piece of crap he and his father had had that argument. It was a betrayal, though. That was what his parents neither understood nor wanted to understand. They were not allowed to use him to get something. That's what everybody else did who had been corrupted by his fame, inspired to make use of it. Just be parents. Go back to ignoring and disparaging him but don't do that and ask exorbitant favours at the same time.

Henry's older brother, Julian, never played the piano. Henry didn't know how he'd done it, but from the earliest age Julian had declared independence, exempting himself from all the music and mawkish, entangling emotion. He'd gone out to play football. Later he'd gone out to drink with his friends by the war memorial.

Later still, he'd got a banking job in Hong Kong and stayed there, starting his own family with Mei and their children and all her relatives.

Childhood piano practice for Henry had felt like today's poor playing. His hands were too small. He was inadequate. And when progress was made, achievement was deferred, the difficulty of the next piece always dancing beyond his fingertips.

He could feel his pulse in his temples. This was too much. Curling up on the sofa he felt like a child. Illness always brought back the sensations of childhood. What came back was that exclusion from the active world, sealed inside his discomfort and slow time. He remembered the sound of the clock, the short nap of the cushion which his face could push one way, smooth, or the other way, a short, upright resilience. TV was not allowed. Books he was allowed but he rarely wanted to read. The quiet of the house occasionally disturbed by a car passing on the road outside, that brief rush of noise, brisk, adult, indifferent, fading quickly into the distance. He heard something like it now, one of the passenger boats that went to Greenwich pushing downriver with a steady churn of engine noise, a long V of wake rasping across the water. This was too much. He switched on the TV. When he was ill and his childhood came back, Henry was preyed on by a thought or a set of images that he didn't like: that all of adulthood was a thin covering, a cheap electroplating, and when it flaked away it revealed what was always underneath, himself as a child. This was precisely what he didn't want to think. No great revelations came with this notion, no key to his personality, no pure effulgence of a spiritual infancy, just the ordinary smallness and miserableness and these meaningless sensations—the feel of a cushion against his face, the sound of a car on a road in the late 1980s, the faint cloudy buzz of noise dislodged from the piano when a heavy lorry went past, the taste of butter on chewy white toast and the brief, unwarranted feeling that something exciting had happened when the street-lamp came on at dusk.

He didn't keep the TV on for long. There were actors out there, many actors who received rewards and adulation for facile tricks that people mistook for good acting. He switched the TV off and became Mike for a moment, tightening his jaw, deadening his eyes. There was a nice crunching feeling when he went into character that was better than anything. It was like his bones turned to cartilage and his shape changed. He put the TV back on again and switched to the classic movie channel. Some cowboys saying aw shucksy things in black and white. He turned the news on and got up to smoke a cigarette.

*

Repetitive days, simple and austere and so bare of incident that they seemed structureless, the hours gaseous and expanding. Still, at any time he could step onto his balcony and see a runner chugging past, or a cormorant by the canal, drying its laundry of wet green wings. In a half-sleep one afternoon, when his thoughts swelled and slurred into dreams, he saw a cormorant very clearly, hunting underwater through the olive gloom, its fixed eye and featherless throat and witchy feathers.

At dusk, the flats around him were reinhabited. He heard muffled noises of other lives, kitchen noises, human and television voices.

During the days he haunted the empty building. He felt like a hallucination, a collective delusion the people in the other flats were having, a daydream while they sat at their desks or in meetings. That was what he was, he realized in a spate of rapid thoughts, standing in the middle of the room with his head full of Mike's lines, that was his task, to be the dream of other people.

*

A wind blew up the river from the North Sea and plastered Henry's coat against his back. A taste of winter when it was barely autumn. And yesterday had been warm with a drowsy, viscous heat. The weather was disordered these days. A mechanism in the sky had broken and bits of different seasons arrived unpredictably, fragmentary, unstable, quickly changing. Possibly he felt the cold more because of his weight. As he walked to the gym people looked at him and there was sometimes the moment of recognition followed by something else, fear or concern.

Henry was too tired to pull the levers of the crosstrainer or haul the stacks of weights. Over time, the hunger had distilled a kind of blackness inside Henry, not a blankness but a positive blackness that throbbed with its own wattage. It stayed behind or at the edge of his vision. It was and was not the same thing as the headaches he suffered. He went to the pool in the basement. Small, dimly lit, it was more of a spa facility than a pool for swimming lengths. The atmosphere was of exclusive calm. The rectangle of water looked plump, like a comfortable mattress, and when Henry got in it lisped over the sides and was recycled back in through some hidden channels. While he was alone he lay face down, listening to the thick silence. The crest of his spine touched the air above. His arms and legs hung down into the water. He thought that García's yes had fallen like a sword across his life. Cut off from everything else and still with no filming date confirmed, Henry had nowhere to go but into himself. He felt his body rock upwards when somebody else got into the pool. Embarrassed, Henry started swimming but only towards the small silver ladder. He climbed out and walked back to the changing room.

*

Henry had been interviewed many times. The danger was to relax, to take the friendliness and keen interest personally. He'd learned that long ago, having said more than he wanted to on several occasions, but he felt himself at risk of doing the same today. A phone interview with an American industry magazine after the full cast had been announced had been sent his way by the production company PR. The journalist was called Patricia. Her American accent, the quietness of her voice, the occasional breath on the mouthpiece or loose rush of laughter felt very intimate in Henry's ear. She sounded very impressed by him. "That's great," she kept saying after his answers. "That's just great."

"Did you know who your co-stars were going to be before this announcement?"

"I didn't actually."

"You must be pretty excited. Sofie Hadermann is such a wonderful actress. Just stunning."

"It's great news. I'm a very lucky actor."

"This is a real breakthrough for you, a very different kind of thing. As I guess it is for anyone going into a García film."

"I guess that's right."

"Are you nervous about it? Nervous about taking on something like this?"

"Oh, no, no. I mean, yes, I'm terrified but not more than I should be. An appropriate level of terror at this point, I think. I can just put my trust in Miguel, you know?"

"Sure, sure. That's great."

"Please don't go with 'Banks Terrified Of Challenge Ahead.'"

"I hadn't thought of that." She laughed, a soft blur of sound, her breath beating on the tiny microphone in the mouthpiece of a phone in Los Angeles. "That's pretty good."

"Do you ever do voiceover work, Patricia?"

"Say again?"

"Do you ever work as a voice artist? You have a nice voice. It's easy money, I tell you."

"Oh. Well, that's another story. Me and acting. Didn't end well. But you know the voice work is actually something my mother has been saying to me for years. It's like a bee in her bonnet she has about it."

"You should listen to your mother."

"Oh, that's cute. Can I ask a personal question?" She lowered her voice. Henry felt a stirring of desire. He had Googled her while they spoke and she was attractive, smart and serious in her by-line photo. In other photos she smiled in the Californian sun. He had her full attention.

"Sure, I suppose. I can always not answer."

"It's just like a biography question. How did you get started? Were you a child actor?"

"I'm disappointed. I was hoping for something more personal than that. I wasn't a child actor but I did discover it then. My parents were both into amateur dramatics for a while. I think you call it community theatre. Like *Waiting for Guffman*-type stuff. So I was involved when I was a kid. I remember loving it immediately, the darkness, the smell of the wings, and then walking out into the light of the stage and straightaway feeling fully, you know, alive out there."

"I do know. I know exactly what you mean."

"I felt it in my spine. I felt I'd found my place in the world."

"Yep."

"One very specific memory from the first time is that someone had spilt some sequins in the wings. This is a bit camp, I guess. I remember spotting them, finding as many as I could, little pieces of light shining in the darkness. It was magical. So that's how it started. I've never actually told anybody that before. You're the first."

"That's sweet. That's more than I need, really."

"Nothing else I can help you with?"

"No, that's it. I've got everything I need now. Have a great day."

"Okay. You, too."

Henry was returned to the silence of the flat. He took his hand from his groin. He looked at his phone for any messages. An email from Carol. A filming schedule, finally? No. Qatar. He'd forgotten about Qatar.

★

As soon as he saw the desert, Henry knew that he was in the right place. It was like no landscape Henry had ever seen before. It was absolute. A place before civilization or after civilization. It was made of sky and nothing, sun and horizon. Henry had seen it as the plane came in to land and glimpsed it now in the car from the airport but very quickly they were facing the skyscrapers of Doha, clustered together in a shimmering group, intricate gold and silver and sheet glass. Like home but a thousand times stranger, like Docklands on acid. Faisal, the guy from the festival who had met him at the airport, explained that Qatar's wealth came from gas. That was the stuff, the vast dinosaur riches, the planetary money that could make a sudden appearance anywhere. Faisal had held Henry's name on a card and a smartphone in his free hand. Narrow-hipped, in black trousers and a white shirt, he smiled eagerly and juggled his objects to shake Henry's hand. His shoes, Henry noticed, were made of some reptile's skin that divided into the rounded squares where scales had been. Faisal smelt fragrantly of aftershave. Seated beside him in the back of the car, he answered Henry's questions. Many of the world's great architects had been brought here to design skyscrapers, attracted by the total creative freedom that had been offered them. The same with the stadiums for the World Cup. Your Lord Norman Foster, for example.

"Is this what Dubai looks like, too?"

"No. It's, well, similar. You haven't been to the Gulf before?"

"Nope."

"Dubai has a different feel. In Qatar they invest in culture a lot, in museums and an orchestra. That sort of thing. And the film festival, the reason you're here."

"I'm culture."

"You are culture."

"And you're not Qatari yourself?"

"Me? No, I'm Egyptian. You won't meet many Qataris, or maybe some with the festival. But they tend to mix with other Qataris. You see that?"

Henry leaned over and looked up at a huge billboard with a sweep of dunes on it and a handsome, moustachioed man wearing the traditional white headcloth thing. Under him, in a flowing font that alluded to Arabic script, ran the title *The Singing Dunes*. Inset on the desert horizon was a silhouette of presumably the same man on horseback.

"This is for your festival."

This was unreal, too real, this emphatic sense of a new place and confirmation of a culture that Henry knew about but did not know. It was always amazing, this failure of the imagination to grasp that things seen on TV and in the papers were actual places a journey away, connected horizontally to where you stand. You had to go there to see. Henry, light-headed from the hours of travel, felt like he was dreaming. After all that time alone, he was avid for these new sensations. He was enthralled when the car swept off the motorway onto a curving drive and into the forecourt of a hotel where uniformed men rushed forward to open the car door and collect his suitcase. Again, for a brief moment, the unmediated air, its heat and stillness. Henry had felt it walking down the staircase from the plane and then again in the moments before he got into the car with Faisal. Again he stepped into a chill downrush of processed air as Faisal led him into the international decor of a five-star hotel lobby and deposited him at reception with his festival information pack. "You don't have to worry about anything," he said while Henry looked around. "I will call you or somebody else from the festival will call you to collect you when you're needed." The place was vast, the central space as high as a shopping mall. Chandeliers hung down over groups of sofas and tables. It took Henry a moment to process how large they were, what a tonnage of crystal was in the air. At one of the tables sat a presumably Qatari couple, the man in a pristine white shirt that hung down to his shining shoes. The checkered cloth on his head was rolled into crested shapes. The woman wore a black dress as dark as her husband's clothes were light. Her face, framed by her headscarf, was perfectly made up. On top of her headscarf rested a pair of Chanel sunglasses. "And all your schedule is in here. All the numbers in case you need anything."

Henry unlocked his door with a swipe of his key and chuckled when he went inside. The room was huge, too. Nice to be in a line of work where you were sud denly picked up by these updrafts of travel and luxury. The bathroom shone with stainless steel and marble. A large shower, big enough for two, provoked the obvious thought of sex. What else were travel and luxury for? He stripped off and used it alone. The pressure was so high it felt like it was sanding the dirt from his body. The shower gel was strongly perfumed, a similar smell to Faisal's aftershave. He had a realization—all the perfumes of Arabia. They must actually be into perfume here. Droplets scattered against the glass glittered in the bathroom's subtle lighting. The water scrubbed at Henry's scalp. He moaned. He dried himself and put on the robe. The television was already on, tuned to an English-language business news channel. A crawl strip of acronyms and numbers moved beneath an

African-American man and a beautiful Asian woman speaking with loud informative friendliness. Outside the air had thickened with dusk. A gritty pink dimness now hung between this building and the others and the traffic circulating below with headlights on. Henry climbed onto his bed with the book he'd been reading on the plane, a memoir by a recent American soldier. He didn't open it, though. He lay back with his head propped on the crisp pillows, the TV remote in his right hand, the book resting on his chest. He had that Arabia perfume now. The pillows were very deep. He felt the hours, the distance draining out of his body.

*

Breakfast was banks and islands of food in a large buffet that needed to be walked around and surveyed before a choice could be made. Some of the food was sculpted. Fruits were sliced and fanned out. Cold meats were folded. Various shapes of bread and pastry, colours of fruit juices and salads, silver barrels of porridge and congee and dhal. There were chefs at a special station for preparing eggs. It would be reasonable just to eat, Henry thought, given that filming still hadn't been announced and he was there for only a couple of days. How much damage could he do? A healthy breakfast could easily be worked off later in the hotel gym. He ladled red berries over yoghurt. He took butter in small fluted curls and a pot of honey to spread over bread rolls. Pastries he still wouldn't allow himself. He took a mango juice and wandered back among the tables.

Henry recognized the back of Philip Townsend's head, the combed sandy schoolboyish hair above the long neck. Philip had played the disgraced politician in *A Paper Fortune*, the film that had long ago written a clause into a contract that demanded Henry's presence at this festival. Tall, weary, ironic, continuously employed playing character roles now that he'd hit his casting in later middle age, Philip was amusing company. "May I?" Henry asked him.

"By all means, old thing."

"And that, my friend, is ridiculous." Henry nodded towards Philip's plate.

"That's a very aggressive start to a conversation."

"Out of all the choices over there, to come away with that."

Philip had in front of him a single as yet unbroached boiled egg in an eggcup.

"I don't have to justify my lifestyle to you. And, really, look at your face. You don't appear to have been gorging yourself."

"Quite the reverse. It's for a role."

"As what? A pencil? A corpse?"

"It's the new Miguel García movie. I'm sort of the lead."

"Don't 'sort of' me. Well, then." Philip weathered this bit of good news with the stoicism of someone who'd been in the business a long time. "That's exciting for you. A biopic about Keira Knightley's body double. It's unusual but then he is the experimental sort." Philip rapped on the top of his egg with his spoon.

"Speaking of which, is Laura here yet?"

"Speaking of what?"

"Attractive women."

"Speaking of which I did a job with your ex Hayley the other day."

"Or let's not speak about it."

"Sorry. I didn't realize."

"It's fine."

Philip absorbed a teaspoon of boiled egg. All his movements were cultured and soft. Henry always felt so macho, so hefty and heavy-handed in his company, and was almost persuaded that he was going about things all wrong. Philip made languid seem the only sensible way to be. In his stillness, his camp, dry Englishness, he gave the impression that the world was performing to amuse specifically him and wasn't doing it terribly well.

"She is here," he said after a moment. "Tweeting away, I expect, or writing some op-ed piece for the *Guardian*."

"I have to say I find feminism very attractive in a woman."

"I think you mean you find Laura Harris very attractive. I may be wrong. Perhaps your hard drive is full of photographs of Andrea Dworkin."

"I don't know who that is but I do have a lot of photos in there so maybe."

"Think a beefier Miriam Margolyes. Important thinker. Your ignorance is shameful."

"But I'm serious. I do like it. It takes guts. Confidence. And what she says is completely reasonable. Equal pay. Equal representation. And the misogyny she gets on social media. It's filthy stuff."

"You should stop writing it, then. She is here, by the way, and you'll be able to express your passionate support to her later."

After breakfast, Henry felt unusually happy. That was the name he gave to the brightness of energy, the painless ease in his body that he hadn't felt for a very long time. He went for a swim in the hotel pool. A flat heat pressed down from above as he made his way around an archipelago of linked areas and back again, beneath the feet of the few people on sun loungers. The sky above the hotel was a brilliant vacancy. The thrill of getting out of London and Britain was the change of light. Henry always noticed it. Away from the sluggish midtones, the whey-white skies, the road greys and brick browns. Out to some Mediterranean sparkle or sharp-shadowed North American winter sunlight or this geographical extreme, the bare furnace of the desert. He became aware of where he was, splashing about in this receptacle of water in this leisure facility improbably placed at the whim of improbable wealth where the planet only burns. He made another circuit and then stood up, sweeping his hair back from his forehead and leaning back with his elbows on the edge. He saw the director of *A Paper Fortune*, Tom, walking to a small table where Laura Harris sat. Henry, his shoulders already instantly dry, submerged again with a shiver and swam towards them. He bounced out of the pool, surging up onto his fingertips, a vertical rush as impressive as he could make it. He picked up the towel from the nearest lounger and cloaked his shoulders. The paving was hot now, though, so he had to return to his own chair with jerky steps to collect his flip-flops. While he was there, he put on his sunglasses and shaped his hair. He went back, carrying his t-shirt in one hand.

"Ay, ay," Henry said.

"Oh, look," Tom said. "It's your co-star. And he has a six-pack, no, an eight-pack."

"Just jealous." Henry pulled on his t-shirt, his display over. "Hi, Laura. How are you?"

Some faces are composed by cameras, aligned and heightened into a beauty that is hard to see in the flesh, but the beauty of some faces is never fully caught on screen. Laura Harris was obviously unusually attractive. Everybody knew that who had seen her image and her work, but the reality of her breathing presence was something else. Henry was used to being among the beautiful. It was in the nature of his profession. Actors were hired in part because they were sexually attractive to the audience. Even if their roles weren't specifically erotic, the audience speculated about having sex with them and discussed their relative attractiveness. Henry was so used to it, in fact, that once or twice out among civilians in London he'd been shocked to see what groups of people looked like when they hadn't been filtered by their appearance, the lumpiness, the dinginess and disarray. The physical beauty of actors was often at odds with their dim or tiresome personalities, but Laura Harris delivered on the promise of her looks. She wasn't thin or tiny. She had a womanly gravity that planted her firmly on the ground. She had shape. She had blond hair and blue eyes and looked like the happiest summer of your life. She had been cast several times for hapless male characters to fall in love with in dramas set in the 1930s and 1950s. One of them, Henry remembered, had several scenes of her riding a bicycle in a translucent summer dress—a cheap decision of the director, one for the dads, as they used to say in light entertainment, but the images were fixed in Henry's mind. And in real life she was intelligent and moral and warm.

"Hey, Henry. You are looking a bit thin there," she said.

"I've had to lose weight for a part."

"Welcome to being an actress."

"Oh, yes," Tom said. "I heard about your good news. Congratulations."

"What's this?"

"Henry's in the new Miguel García project, aren't you?"

"I am. At least I will be when it finally starts filming."

"Did you get to meet him?"

"I did, of course."

"And what's he like?"

"There's a lot of myth around him, I know. In person he's perfectly nice. Scarily clever, obviously. We looked at paintings together in the National Gallery."

"Wow. What was that about?"

"I'm going to have to leave you two to this discussion," Tom said. "I've got a Skype meeting to attend. Trying to get this Somerset Maugham adaptation finally off the ground. I'll see you later for our scheduled boat ride. We're getting all the tourist treats."

"Oh, sure. See you then."

Tom had clearly heard enough about another director's brilliance. He padded away and back into the hotel. Small and freckled and vulnerable under the drenching sun, he wore a straw trilby for protection.

"It was pretty great," Henry said. "We looked at a Velázquez, I can never say that word, painting and talked about suffering and art and religion. All these things are in the film on some level."

"Fantastic."

"So that's my big news. What about you? I've been following your various campaigns. Signed a few petitions that came round. I don't do Twitter myself but I've seen what you've be doing, fighting the good fight."

Laura leaned forward to scratch her shin. "You're better off out of it with Twitter. It ranges from okay to dispiriting to out and out vile. Being on there in possession of a vagina can get pretty scary, I can tell you."

"A vagina. I've heard of those. You're in possession of one?"

"Yep, and lots of guys on the internet have lots of plans for it, it turns out. Quite a few want to make use of it before or after they kill me."

"Jesus. It is horrendous. This conversation has taken a dark turn here."

"That's what it's like online. Instant escalation. Zero to rape threats in three seconds."

"Well, I do really admire you for doing it. I mean that."

"Thanks. It's not all bad, don't worry. There are also a lot of men who want to buy me specific kinds of underwear and / or marry me."

"Now that I can understand. I had a destined-to-marry-me one the other day—even without social media they find a way. My agent is supposed to stop them getting to me but somehow this one slipped through."

"Maybe it's because she—it is a she, yes?—is destined to marry you?"

"That's a good point. I might need to think about this a bit more."

A pause in the conversation. Henry did indeed think about the woman who had written the letter, out there someplace unknown, thinking of him. The slap of water in the pool. The drone of an aircraft. A waiter carried drinks misted with condensation to another table then tucked his tray under his arm and turned to them.

"Can I bring you anything?" He leaned towards them and his posture froze, waiting for a response. He was bald, his head bright in the sun. He squinted.

"I don't want anything," Henry said. "Do you?"

"Not right now."

"Nothing for us," Henry said and the waiter returned to his station. "This is kind of a weird place to be, isn't it? A bit sort of sinister, in a way."

"I suppose."

"You think I'm being racist?"

"Scared of Arabs?"

Henry looked around at the water. "I guess I am a bit. We are in quite a lively neighbourhood. News from this part of the world doesn't tend to be the most reassuring."

"I'm not going to disagree, in a way. I'm not sure I'd be here if it weren't in the contract. Workers live in labour camps over here. Did you see them, Bangladeshis and Nepalis, out on the building sites on the way from the airport? They die all the time in accidents. They have to work in this insane heat."

"Just terrible."

Laura laughed. "You sound really concerned. That's nice."

"That's not fair. I think it's terrible."

"But you hadn't thought about it before. I bet you hadn't even noticed the brown people out there doing the dangerous work. You were talking about them darn terrorists."

"No, I wasn't."

"No one's going to behead you here. But sure as shit Qatari money is going into the conflicts. They're all over the region in different ways. They fund Al Jazeera, too, you know? It's based here."

"I did know that, as it happens."

"But to answer your underlying question, you're safe. The waiter just wanted to bring you a pomegranate juice."

"Oh, good. I thought he was asking if we wanted to star in a beheading video."

"Only you would think of 'starring' in a beheading movie. I think he's safe. You're not frightened of these people, are you?" She pointed discreetly, a quick dart of her finger across her chest. Henry looked around at a family group that had assembled on loungers by the pool, a father sitting next to his son, both wearing swimming trunks. The mother, swathed in cloth, sat upright on a chair. Something about the boy slowed Henry's attention, something different. Oh, that was it, the boy had Down's syndrome—the smoothness and roundness of his face, the soft, entirely unself-conscious body. He was adjusting the strap of a diving mask while his father smeared sun cream on his back. The father had a curly wreath of hair around a bald patch, hair on his chest and the slope of his belly. The mother was talking to them both. Henry marvelled at them. He had the strange sensation that Laura had magicked them into being, or at least allowed him to see them. Laura's essential bias, despite all she went through with her campaigning, was to like and trust people and the result seemed to be that good, warm, human people came into view around her. She made Henry feel like a better person.

"I'm not very frightened," Henry said. "Depends what he's planning to do when he's got that mask on."

Laura, her expression soft as she gazed at them, said, "Cute."

Henry looked at Laura looking. He said, "This is nice. I've been shut up on my own for a while. It's nice to make contact again."

Laura said, "Sure it is."

She looked like a life, a calm and decent way to be.

★

Henry returned to the hotel buffet for lunch with an eager appetite. He took rice pilaf with slices of toasted almonds and bright gems of pomegranate seeds that burst in his mouth with sharp, lush flavour. He ate chicken that was charred at the edges from the grill, pulling the flesh from the bones with his fork. He swept rags of flatbread through the sumptuous gloop of hummus and baba ghanoush. He ate some mysterious cream for dessert that was flavoured with cardamom and had a savoury green grit of crushed pistachios sprinkled on top.

He ate until he was full. Henry felt pleasure back inside his body, the enlivening effects of sugar and sunlight. He felt strong enough for his glorious future.

★

The skyscrapers needed cooling and the gardens all had to be watered, the new stadiums, all that acreage of grass and mass of air conditioning: the need for water was tremendous. The desalination plants were being enlarged. Already the water in the Gulf was thickening, its salt content killing some of the fish. Faisal was on the boat with them explaining all of this. Henry looked at a dhow floating in front of them, at a fisherman walking sure-footed along its length. A lyrical, Arabian sight. He responded to what Faisal was telling him with small sounds of deprecation. This was being a tourist in the modern world, enjoying the view while knowing the water was poisoned, the sea overfished and the sea level rising. Among educated people this might be the topic of conversation, too, at least for a while, a little geopolitical mournfulness between forgetful pleasures. Faisal turned their attention to the Museum of Islamic Art, built on a specially constructed island at the request of its famous architect. Henry hadn't heard of him but Faisal explained it was the man responsible for the glass pyramid at the Louvre which everyone knew. The museum was plain and elegantly geometric. It rose impressively above the water. To Henry it looked like something from the distant past as much as from the far future. That was clever. It was a religious building, after all, expressing a permanent authority.

Henry said to Laura, "Nice to have a change of scene now and again."

"Hmm," she replied.

Being on a boat made pauses in the conversation natural and meditative. They looked out across the expanse of water.

"Nice to be ferried around," he said.

"Do you ever get the feeling," she said, "that we're just a little ornament of the capitalist system?"

"Sure."

"It's corporate money that's ferrying us around because we entertain."

"Kind of. We're jesters. Sure. I know that. We're culture."

"Unlike the Bangladeshis."

"But you can change things. You do charity stuff and campaign and make people think."

"I try."

"Is this how you flirt, by the way, heavy political conversation?"

"No," Laura said. "Just occurred to me."

"I see."

They lapsed into silence for a moment. Henry said, "How do you flirt?"

Laura laughed. "I saw your ex the other day. Hayley."

"Oh, did you?" What was this? Was she pushing him away, telling him that she knew the case against him, or was she testing him? He asked, "And how is she?"

"She's well."

"That's good to hear. I still miss her."

"Do you?"

"I do. But what can you do? Maybe you need these things to happen, you know, to grow. I think it's helped me grow as a person, I really do."

"I see," Laura said. "Well, that's something."

*

After their excursion on the boat, they had been returned to the hotel to prepare for the official opening of the festival. Henry had brought with him a narrow black tie rather than a bow tie to go with his sharply cut dinner suit. After a shower, he dressed slowly and carefully like he was building something, fitting the parts together. The knotting of his tie was the final act of assembly. He tightened his cheeks slightly and angled his head. The mirror showed him the perfect image of a man, like looking at a page in a magazine. He hoped that the film would move him up into the category of star that is used to sell watches and aftershave and cars. How's that for a jester for capitalism, he thought and made the single-finger gun gesture at himself in the mirror. Think of Kate Winslet and George Clooney wearing wrist-watches and staring into the distance, earning millions for an afternoon's work. And what was it Beyoncé sold in those black and white photos with her heavy, erotic, sphinx's stare? Pepsi, wasn't it? Nothing wrong with it. Someone's going to be asked and who in their right mind would refuse? If you want to spend the money on good causes then go for it.

Simplified inside the diagram of his suit, eager and alert, his face feeling smart with the after-effects of the sun, Henry met the others in the lobby and got into the transport to the venue.

There were fewer photographers than there would have been in London and these ones were polite, used to serving the obedient press of a rich, non-democratic country. The guests passed in front of the festival brand-ing and stood in the spasming light, looking into each lens in turn. Laura wore a blue silk shoulderless dress, a spiral of fabric from which she seemed to be rising, naked. Her hair hung in heavy lacquered shapes. Henry stood beside her and angled his head for the photographs. Behind them Philip pursed his lips and lifted his chin.

The carpet then led them onto a terrace where other people stood in soft lighting, laughing and talk-ing. Above them the desert sky was darkening. Waiters circulated with drinks. Henry took one. A delicate fla-vour of mint and rose, Islamically innocent of alco-hol. At one edge of the terrace a string quartet played, their intricate music floating away, ignored. The air was warm. Every point of contact with the world was soft and expensive, designed for enjoyment. Henry didn't recognize many people here and the hierarchies were obscure, to be discerned from the attitudes and distribution of the people. There was much alert and willing laughter around an Indian actor wearing a collarless shirt of ochre silk and a large silver watch. He looked almost familiar. Qatari aristocrats wore their brilliant white shirts under black, gold-edged cloaks. Together, Henry, Laura, Philip and Tom circulated around the space, observing, commenting, talking to each other for company, at least until Tom was called away by a loud and friendly voice. Beyond the edge of the terrace, the sea was dim but for one area where it reflected the lights of the skyscrapers.

A small, white-suited man appeared at Henry's side and said in a clear English voice, "You don't know me but I know you. My wife is a big fan of *The Grange*. How are you liking Doha?" He held a glass in one hand and gripped his elbow with the other, a tightly folded, interrogative posture. He had an artistic, tousled quiff and stylish glasses. He smiled up at Henry.

"Amazing place," Henry said. "It's all been very comfortable. How do you like it?"

"Oh, you know. After a while it gets a little dull. There isn't that much to do until exciting people like you come to town. I'm here for work."

The man, whose name was Peter something, was an architect and ran a firm that was responsible for an extensive new area in Doha, restaurants and retail, intended to meet the demand of the influx of people for the World Cup. He was interesting enough. Henry spoke to him with friendliness and animation. This

89

was the way with these events: they threw people your way and you enjoyed them as far as you could before they were gone. Peter something moved on saying, "I really shouldn't monopolize you. There will be loads of people wanting to talk to you." The terrace was now filled with people. The talk and the music were a noise that enveloped them. The photographers had finished at the red carpet and moved among them, shooting.

Laura appeared by Henry and said, "Come and see this pretty pond."

"Pretty pond?"

"That's what I said."

He followed her bare shoulders to a small circular pond with flowers and candles floating in it.

"Very nice," he said. "But who do you have to fuck around here to get a proper drink?"

"Don't think that's on the cards," she said.

"Which bit?"

"Come on. Philip is giving me that look of please get me out of this conversation."

A number of similar and beautiful women appeared in a line towards a door. An announcement was made in Arabic and English that the evening was about to begin inside. The women, the models, were deployed like traffic cones to guide the guests into the hall.

Seated at the table for *A Paper Fortune*, surveying the room, hearing the chinking noises of organized catering behind a door, seeing the large screen behind the podium with its festival logo and the burst of flowers on either side, Henry prepared himself for hours of ceremonial boredom. And this time the event would unfold with the comfortless clarity of forced sobriety. Still, it should be shorter than the television awards he had sat through, long evenings of tedium and misbehaviour and one, when he had been nominated, of adrenalin and misery, seeing his face appear on the screen for one hot minute, composing his face to applaud when the winner stood up beaming, strenuously kissed his beautiful wife and ran up the stairs to make his speech.

On Henry's right was Tom, reading the menu card thoroughly. Beyond him, Laura sat, out of conversational reach, sipping a glass of water. On Henry's left, Philip Townsend arranged himself for detached observation, his legs crossed, his large hands holding his knees. "Look out," he said. "Time to Sheikh Yerbouti."

A Qatari man, holding his cloak with one hand and papers in the other, climbed to the podium and waited through a burst of fanfaring music and a swirl of animated logo on the screen behind. When he spoke, Henry was fascinated by the gutturals and glottal stops, the harsh, commanding sound of his Arabic. The effect was dispelled when he translated the warm, bland words of greeting into English tinged with an American accent. Other speeches followed, a VT package with many swooping, overhead shots of Doha filmed either from a helicopter or a drone, the flying logo again, clips from the festival's films. It was over sooner than Henry had feared. The end released applause around the room, a sound of relief, prolonged for courtesy. Before it was over, the waiters were flowing between the tables to deliver something the menu card called a cappuccino of bouillon, a thin, salty heat that was soon spooned away—but already the waiters were returning to remove the cups and deliver a chef's version of the now familiar Arabic hors d'oeuvres. The noise of talk and clattering ceramics made it hard to hear across the table. Henry gave up trying to join in Laura's conversation with Tom. The back of the director's head confronted Henry who could hear the shape of his words but not what they were, likewise the rapid tune of Laura's replies. He turned to Philip, who was staring across the room. Henry followed the line of his gaze to find a handsome waiter smiling back.

"Have you pulled already?" Henry asked him.

"So vulgar," Philip said. "But you might be right. Further research necessary, as they say." He beckoned the waiter over.

"So bloody easy for you people," Henry said. "It's just not fair."

Henry ate flavoured rice and cubes of lamb while the waiter bent his ear close to Philip's moving lips, to anyone observing apparently taking an order. The waiter straightened and nodded, looked around him and left.

"All done," Philip said. "Boredom and thoughts of death evaded for another night."

"Just taking it one day at a time, taking it where you can find it."

After the main course, Tom announced, "I'm going out for a cigarette."

"Have you got a spare?" Henry asked him.

"I can probably loan you one. Probably my last chance to smoke with a future A-lister."

"Great."

They stood up and walked through the diners, the suits and dresses, the hairstyles and jewellery and faces, and out through a heavy door which, closing behind them, bottled the noise of the room. They were away in another dimension, escaped. They followed the corridor to the exit and found it attended by one of the traffic cone models, alone, pacing a few steps back and forth with her long arms folded, half dancing, dipping and swinging her feet. When she saw them she was still suddenly and smiled a wide professional smile. Henry said to her, "Is this the way out?"

"It certainly is," she replied.

"You're American," he said.

"You're observant. And I know who you are, Dr. McAlister."

"Real name's Henry."

"Well, it's just through here, Henry."

Tom, ignored, went impatiently through the door while Henry lingered.

"What's your name?"

"Virginia. I'm Virginia. But I'm from Kentucky."

"Virginia from Kentucky. We're just going out for a cigarette."

"Those things'll kill you, you know."

"I do. But tobacco's one of my five a day, so ... I'll catch you later or he'll be finished before I get a smoke."

On the terrace, Tom said, "You just can't help yourself. Just oozing charm."

"I was just being friendly. I was being polite. Now give us a fag."

Tom reached into his jacket and pulled out a packet of Benson and Hedges.

"Thank you kindly."

The paper cylinder with its dry fragrance. The bobbling flame from his lighter. The first drag. The large warm night around them. "God, I'm full of food," Henry said. "It's gonna be a horrible purge when I get back."

"Go to the gym at the hotel. Burn it off."

"But I'm on me holidays."

Tom inhaled, exhaled a blue plume upwards towards the stars.

"So you and Laura seemed deep in conversation," Henry said.

"We were. It's my desperation getting the better of me."

"Out of your league, mate. Out of everybody's league."

"No, not her. Her boyfriend. You know she goes out with Josh Rappaport, the writer. You know him?"

"Think I met him once." Curly hair, black-framed glasses, the sly kind of self-confidence that masquerades as witty self-deprecation.

"His hit rate is just, you know. He's just a phenomenal writer, I think. And he has an unattached screenplay sitting in his drawer, I happen to know, and I want it bad."

Henry dragged hard on his cigarette. It was interesting the way you could tell physically that some people were second-rate. Tom with his pale neck, his small hands and imprecise gestures, smoking with little popping noises of his lips, desiring this script he wouldn't get to see, was second-rate. Henry felt a very focused hatred of Tom and the sound of his voice (still talking about this script) that protected him momentarily from his misery. Laura was out of his reach. The better life, the better person he could be, unobtainable. Of course she was going out with someone like Josh Rappaport. Of course she wouldn't be interested in Henry who was just another actor, after all. Without her saying a word, Henry felt summarized and judged. Henry was not good enough.

"Shall we go back in?" he said.

"I suppose we must."

Opening the door of the banqueting room and stepping in, Henry was overwhelmed by a gale of trivial sound, clattered plates and loud, blended voices. The waiters swirled among the seated guests whose carefully composed looks were now loosening a little, heated, moderately disarranged. Henry sat back down and leaned behind Tom's chair to Laura.

"So your partner's Josh Rappaport?" he said.

"That's right."

"Must be nice for you. A writer like that. Like having an oil well in your garden."

Laura laughed. "That's one way of looking at it. Still waiting for him to write me a big part."

There was a plate of dessert in front of Henry, a rectangle of some sort of mousse, a long line of caramel, dots of some other sauce, a crisp made from fruit. Henry demolished its pretty geometry with the side of his spoon.

After the plates were cleared and the coffee delivered, there was more activity at the podium. The evening was not over yet, as Henry would have known if he'd read with any attention the emails he'd been sent and the festival pack in his hotel room. They were a short walk away from the cinema where the opening film of the festival, *The Singing Dunes*, would be shown.

Henry drank his coffee. He had no steady estimation of himself. As the crowd rose and dispersed, he felt himself miserable and shrivelled and separate among them, Laura rising out of her dress at a great and final distance. The only thing for it was to go on and play his role with García and become so successful that it almost didn't matter. How many of these people at this backwater festival had ever met Miguel García? The future was clear and obvious. The present counted for nothing—it crumbled away in the movement around him of many irrelevant people.

They were all outside for a moment, improbable in their outfits, the women holding parts of their clothing that were insecure in the breeze or would trail along the ground. They walked along a path marked by flames in glass jars and the standing models. Henry sought Virginia's face on top of one of the tall and narrow bodies but didn't find her until they were inside the next building.

"Hey, Virginia," he said.

"Hello, Doctor."

"Will you be here later?"

"It's in my job description."

"Can I come out and find you a bit later?"

"I'm not allowed to move."

"Perfect."

"Enjoy the film."

"I may come out during the film."

"Okay."

Long minutes of settling in the cinema preceded more bombastic festival idents, this time booming through a full Dolby sound system. Henry's sense of recognition as the title sequence unfolded became a memory of the billboard he had seen on the way from the airport. That felt like a long time ago, although it was hardly more than a day.

The Singing Dunes clearly had artistic ambitions. It opened with long, moodily composed shots of sand dunes, a fine spittle of sand flying from their tops, resonating with a strange thrumming sound. Differently shadowed forms, natural sculptures, formed over geological eons, Henry was absorbed by them although, still irritable, he thought that "singing" was going a bit far. They buzzed with a meaningless noise, the by-product of physical circumstances. Henry found watching them relaxing, a relief, clean, empty, sombre and strange. But then a new shot: an indistinct shape seen through the gelatinous distortions of heat haze got larger and came into focus, a horseman getting closer, thundering past the camera. An epic romance began. The horsemen multiplied. There were battles and revenge sworn and sunsets and shy, beautiful women, a whole human pre-posterousness laid over the dead landscape. A truly foreign sensibility was at work that looked naïve to Henry, earnest heavy-handedness made the dramatic turning points emphatic, the score was surging and orchestral. Henry got up as if to use the bathroom and muttered apologies as he edged out of his row.

Virginia wasn't where he'd last seen her. He asked another of the girls where she was.

"Who is she?" she asked.

"You're Russian," he said.

"I'm Ukrainian."

"Okay. Sorry. Virginia. She's an American girl."

"Yes. I think she is this way." She pointed along the sloping corridor. "I am the guard." She smiled. "Everyone else is in the big room."

Henry jogged up the corridor to the foyer where he found several of the models sitting on gold-painted chairs, chatting, looking at their phones. They looked up at him as he entered. "Hey. Hi," he said. "I'm look-ing …" Virginia stood up.

"Over here," she said and beckoned with a scooping hand. He jogged over. It was like a game played around the house at Christmas, like hide and seek. They stood close to the wall for privacy, speaking quietly, their faces close together.

"So when the cars come afterwards," Henry said, "you just get into mine with me. We'll go together. There's a bar with actual drink drinks at my hotel."

"Are you, sir, offering me alcohol?"

"I am."

"I could get into trouble. I mean actual trouble for, like, abandoning my post or whatever."

"You won't. I'll take the blame. We'll say you were helping me with a medical emergency."

"What emergency?"

"Fatal attraction."

She laughed. "That's so ridiculous." Henry laughed, too, lighthearted, genuinely amused by their conspiracy by the patterned wallpaper.

"Great. Excellent. I'll see you when this bullshit's over, then."

Henry put a hand on her shoulder and squeezed, then hurried back down to the cinema.

*

"Holy shit. Your hotel is so much grander than ours."

"We're talent. We're the hot cultural commodity."

"And we're flight attendants is what it feels like."

"Still, I bet yours is better than what the Bangladeshis and Nepalis are in, the guys building this place. They live in actual labour camps apparently."

"That's no good."

"I know. Check out those chandeliers."

Virginia looked up into the vast hotel atrium. She said, "I'm not sure you really care about the workers."

"I care. I do charity work. I care. I mean, if they just pulled their fingers out and developed some basic acting skills they could be in here rather than out there. If they just put on the odd production of *Twelfth Night* instead of building football stadiums the whole time. Bit of initiative, that's all."

"You're a bad man."

"That's right. Okay, I need to find out where this bar is."

Henry drank Old Fashioneds, Virginia vodka and tonic. Her mouth was large, her eyes widely spaced and staring. She had a fashion model's looks, just this side of grotesque, alarmingly beautiful. When she smiled, curving lines flexed from the sides of her mouth to the apples of her cheeks. Her wrists and hands were long and gave the impression of an unused excess of dexterity when she handled her glass and drinking straw. Henry said to her, "So what goes on in Virginia?"

"Say what now?"

"I'm sorry. I actually made that mistake. What goes on in Kentucky?"

"Oh there. Not too much. That's why I moved up to New York."

"You live in New York."

"Well, Queens. You have to be there for all the castings, the shows, for everything. Weird gigs like this one. So freakin' expensive, though. I live in a models' apartment, as in we're all models. When I tell guys this they usually get excited but it's really not like you'd like it to be. It's a lot of arguing about bathroom access and underwear on all the radiators and a depressing kitchen with a refrigerator where everyone keeps like three out-of-date yogurts."

"Do you want to come and see my room? I bet it's better than your room in Queens."

"You mean just like survey it in a real estate way. For comparison."

"Exactly. Let's go."

"You're not hanging around."

"Ooh. The world feels different when you get off the stool."

"Just hold my arm, you'll be fine."

On the way to the elevator Henry's pocket buzzed. Emails. His phone had reconnected to the hotel's wifi. He took it out and checked. "What's that?" Virginia said. "Fan mail?"

"If only." There was one from his mother. *Henry, I'm sure you're very busy but if you could just find five minutes.*

Henry said to Virginia, "Do you know if you can legally divorce your parents?"

"Just walk away, Henry. You don't need lawyers. Out the front door and keep going."

*

"My God, the rooms, too. This is just unfair."

"It does the job."

"Two beds, like a queen double situation. This is great. It'll be like summer camp. We can lie on our separate beds and tell each other secrets."

"Great. So you're staying, then? Let's take our clothes off and roll around."

"That didn't happen at my summer camp."

"Things have moved on since … don't even tell me when. It's going to be way too recent."

"Okay, mister." She walked towards him. "If we're going to do this."

The first drunken kiss, one of life's reliable pleasures.

Virginia's body looked lonely. Was that the word? Long and narrow with small projecting breasts and no pubic hair and shadows between her ribs. A very exposed body, a working body. Henry could see it stepping in and out of clothes, posing, makeup applied and cleansed away, chemicals to style her hair, a body scoured by other people's attention, by the impacts of photographs. He felt for her. This was something that seemed to have come with age, the ability to see the human person even in this moment. The moment passed, though. The feminine shapes, the willing contact overwhelmed him. He experienced the secret pleasure that he had with someone new, conquest, possession gained watching her give in and do what he wanted. It felt almost like a theft from her that she would never know about. It happened as they began on the bed, looking down at her face, then passed as things became focused on small adjustments to avoid discomfort, intimate, and then strenuous and obliterating. At least for him. When he was close he looked down at her face to check and she said, "Don't worry about me. It's okay."

"But ..."

And then quietly, perhaps knowing that it would send him quickly over the edge, "Don't worry. You can just fuck me."

Afterwards, they showered together the parts of their bodies that needed cleaning, making use of the large and sparkling bathroom, living up to its promise. Dry again, Virginia wearing a robe, Henry wrapped in a thick towel, returning to the bedroom after all the frenzy, they felt sexless and innocent. They climbed into bed like children, kicking the huge crackling duvet loose and pulling it up under their chins, showing each other only their silly faces.

"Thanks for staying over with me, Kentucky."

"Oh, you're welcome."

"And so well brought up."

"Not exactly."

"So," Henry was interested in her now. "Is modelling what you want to do? In life?"

"In life? Not really. It doesn't last anyway. I take photographs. I have a Tumblr of my pictures."

"Cool. I'll look it up."

"I want to study, really. Go to college. If there's some way it won't bankrupt me."

"You should do that. You're obviously smart."

"Patronizing much?"

"Hey, I'm showing you my good side right now. Take it while you can get it."

"Good night, Dr. McAlister." She leaned forwards and kissed the tip of his nose.

"Don't call me that. I'm trying to leave that dude behind."

"Never watched it myself. But my mom loved that show. Loved it. Spoke about the characters like they were real people. You'll never guess what Dr. McAlister said."

"Always the way with that show. People's mothers watched it. Or their wives. Never them. Hey, did I tell you I've got this amazing new part in a big movie?"

"Well, that's just tremendous."

"That's why I'm so thin."

"Not in my world you're not."

"I'm pleased you're here with me."

"You said that already."

"Goodnight, Kentucky."
"Goodnight, England."

★

Henry didn't sleep well. He was unused to having someone else in the room. He drifted up to the surface of consciousness several times, aware of the dimly visible room.
Even so, when he was woken by an electronic noise that
wouldn't stop, it took him some moments to work out
that the strange mass of hair and shoulder blades in front
of him was Virginia and the noise was coming from her
phone. He reached out and touched her back with the
flat of his hand. She flinched. "Oh, I'm sorry," she said
and typed the alarm off with a jabbing finger. "I'm sorry. I
have to get back to my hotel. I have to get back to work."

"But it's so early."

"I'm sorry."

"It's okay. I'll come down with you. We'll get some
breakfast in the buffet."

"Okay. Nice man."

As only one breakfast was allotted to his room number, Henry had to add Virginia's to his bill. It hardly
seemed worth the flat tariff when she took only black
coffee, a glass of water and two slices of watermelon.

"That's what I should be having," he told her, sipping a berry smoothie, a bowl of granola and a plate of
scrambled eggs in front of him.

"It's food," she said, eating a pink square from her
fork, "without any of the downsides of food." She ate it
quickly, slicing different bite-sized shapes with her knife
and fork. "I've got to go. Otherwise they'll put out an
alert. Actually, they probably wouldn't."

"Get a cab at reception and put it on my room number."

"I think they'll need you to sign off."

"You've done this before."

"Don't be rude."

"I'll come with you, don't worry."

They went out to the lobby together. Henry ordered her cab. He kissed her cheek. "I'll find you later."

"Okay. Sure. I'll be there."

"What? So will I. That's what I'm saying."

"Kissing me on the cheek like that."

"What? You want to French kiss? I'm being sensitive to local customs."

"Sure you were."

The things that women found significant, their interpretations. And always new ones, things you couldn't predict. "I was," he said.

"Okay. Now go before your eggs get cold."

Philip appeared beside him as he walked back to the dining area. "You've made a friend, I see."

"I did. A model. American."

"Congratulations. Have you seen that media person, whatever she's called? She's supposed to be wrangling us into the interview booth."

"Oh, goody."

"Oh, you love it."

"For about ten minutes. Why don't you help yourself to some food? I'll eat whatever these leftovers are."

★

Seated in front of the posters for *A Paper Fortune*, with plastic bottles of mineral water on hand and tea and coffee brought by hurrying festival assistants, Tom and Laura and Philip and Henry in varying combinations faced the different interviewers. Before they went in Tom reminded them the key ideas to hit in their answers and things in the plot they couldn't reveal. The latter was fine by Henry. He could hardly remember what happened in the scenes—most of the film—in which he didn't appear.

"In we get," Philip said. "Nice warm bath of smarm."

It was an exercise in synthesized enthusiasm, in mild flirtation and dissembled boredom and joke making, in responding to the quirky novelty questions that one of the interviewers asked. If you were a Muppet which Muppet would you be? *Star Wars* or *Star Trek*? These were asked by a young man from a Lebanese TV station who wore an outsized plastic red watch that inspired Philip to ask drily, "Do you have the time?" and later, "Do we have time, do you think, for any more questions?"

A more reflective interview was conducted by an older Arabic cinephile who spoke in a low growl, wore square plastic-framed glasses and whose face of heavy stippled flesh looked cured in cigarette smoke. He sat back in his chair, the shoulders of his jacket rising to his ears. "Miss Harris, you are looking very beautiful," he said.

Laura murmured something in reply.

"Don't deny it," Henry said. "You are."

"And what about me?" Philip asked.

"Not as beautiful as you, obviously," Henry said.

The interviewer seemed perplexed. He began reading from his list of questions about this not entirely successful, meat-and-potatoes British political thriller. He looked as though he would be happier discussing Jean-Luc Godard or Abbas Kiarostami and asked questions that were more interesting than the film. He asked

Laura about the female character as a sort of moral beacon and wasn't that a regressive archetype in a way and Laura agreed, as far as she could within the bounds of promoting the film. He asked Henry about the prospect of working with the great Miguel García, an auteur, a provocateur. He'd done his research, evidently.

Henry responded with how excited and nervous he was, what an inspirational artist García was, even just meeting him. Philip interrupted. "Shouldn't we stick to the film here at the festival?"

"Indeed, indeed." He asked a few more questions then switched off his Dictaphone and made his farewell. He shook Henry and Philip's hand and gave Laura a gentlemanly but no doubt relished kiss on the cheek. When he'd gone and the assistant was back offering more bottles of water, Laura said to Henry, "You must be getting pretty excited about that job now. Don't you start rehearsing next week?"

"I don't think I do. Not that I know."

"I'd check with your agent. I got a text from my friend, Tess. She's second AD-ing. I'm sure that's what she said."

"Are you sure you're sure?"

"Yep. Here it is. Look. Rehearsing next week. Filming two weeks after that."

"I think I need to go and call my agent."

As he left, he raised reassuring hands at the media coordinator's questioning face. "Five minutes. I'll be back."

★

"It's fine. Don't worry."

"Carol, it's so soon."

"But you're flying back tomorrow. It's rehearsal. Don't panic."

106

"I just would have liked to know sooner is the only thing."

"Henry, I understand. We only got the information like ten minutes ago."

In the bathroom, fear drained the strength out of him, pulled the breath from him, tossed him into a cubicle to vomit. That almost felt like a choice, like the best thing he could do to alleviate his state. After a painful dry wrenching of internal muscles, it splashed out bright pink. It took Henry a frightened moment to connect this with his breakfast smoothie. The retching started again of its own accord, jerking his chin down towards the pan, flushing involuntary tears from the sides of his eyes. When it was over and he'd flushed it away and had pressed cold water to his face, he felt feeble and quiet, quietly scared, like a small animal.

García had extended Henry the greatest invitation to failure he could imagine. That was suddenly clear. He might not be able to do it. Why did he think he could? He could fail terminally and everything that he wanted to happen then would not. But it was coming. There was no way out of it. There was nothing he could do.

He returned to the interview room for two more. He said almost nothing, looking across at Laura whenever a question was asked so that she would answer while his thoughts looped in tightening circles.

He ignored lunch. He went outside into the simplifying heat, the burning elegant surfaces of the architecture. He tried to remember everything he knew about Mike and to become him just for a moment, to feel the softening and then the new structures forming. He almost could but not really. If he forced it, he would become a cartoon of Mike, stiff and superficial.

There was the ceremony of *A Paper Fortune*'s screening now to go through. Applause. Standing up front smiling humbly while the director said a few words. In the dark, he had to watch himself. Lumpen, untransformed, inadequate in a film that was barely adequate. In one exchange he hit something, something snapped into place with a sharp, rhythmical line reading. And he didn't even have a memory of that moment. His empty stomach simmered. He wanted to get up out of his seat. He wanted to fuck Virginia again. He wanted to run. When it was over, there was more applause and then in the crush outside several short conversations to have with members of the audience. Through the throng, he could see Virginia giving directions to someone. When she was free, she came over to him.

"You were great," she said.

"You were in there?"

"I got in."

"Anyway, I beg to differ."

"Don't be modest."

"I'm not. I really want to get out of here."

"Later on we can. I've found the party."

"What do you mean?"

"For tonight. One of the local Qatari guys, a younger one, is having a thing at his house and he's invited like all the models. You can come with. We can get our crazy on."

"That's good. That's good. I'd like to blow my brains out with fun. I'm so pleased I met you."

*

"These cars are ridiculous," Henry said as a white Mercedes SUV collected several more of the girls.

"All those luxury cars you see driving around," Virginia said. "Those are the Qataris. You know they get like a hundred grand each from the government per year just for being Qatari. At least."

"Benefits scum. That's a British joke. Welfare queens, you'd say. Are you sure they really want me there?"

"Sure they do. You're famous. Your bringing the glamour, baby."

"I think that's your job."

"Probably all their moms watch *The Grange*."

Sitting next to each other in the back of a Range Rover, they surged smoothly through the nighttime city and out to a private residence where girls were being unloaded from another car. Two of them were laughing, talking in some Slavic language as they approached the house. A servant admitted them. The host stood behind, smiling and welcoming, his muscular torso packed into a tight, neatly torn t-shirt. He seemed pleased to see them. He looked happy, Henry thought, relieved from boredom, bright with the pleasure of acquisition. Henry recognized that look—hopeful, permissive, impersonal—and sympathized. It was the right spirit to start a party. Henry shook the host's hand, a strong clamp that flexed the man's bicep, and smelled his aftershave as he passed.

The house was made of large spaces, softly lit. There were brass objects, pots and the like, massive leather furniture, fabrics hanging on the walls.

"Very desert chic," Henry said. He put on a gay interior designer's voice. "I love it."

A massive kitchen with a three-sided breakfast bar was full of food and drink. Beyond, through a wall of glass, was an inner courtyard. Henry walked out into it.

There was a large marble pond. Henry, pulling Virginia with him, went to look: turning slow gold shapes of carp, a small trickling fountain. While they were out there music started with a thump of speaker noise. A music system of shockingly high definition and volume got the party started. Henry could feel a breeze coming from the bass.

A waiter appeared with a tray of drinks. Virginia took two, handed one to Henry.

"Thank you." He leaned to her ear to be heard. "What is it?"

"One way to find out."

They drank some. "I still don't know," Henry said, pulling a mint leaf from his lip. "But it is booze. Let's do more walk-around. You haven't introduced me to any of your model friends."

"I don't know them. I should go and talk to Marta. She was kind of assaulted by one of your people last night."

"My people?"

"A famous."

On the way, Henry's arm was held. He was detached from Virginia who carried on. The grip belonged to a short man who said, "Can I just ask you something real quick? Are you that guy from that British show?"

"I might be."

"I thought it was you."

"And who are you?"

"I am Ilham."

"Il—what is that?"

"Il*ham*. I work with Daoud. We are making a record company."

"This is his house?"

110

"Yes, yes."

Henry stayed for a while in this eddy of conversation, catching another drink as it floated past.

After another hour or so, there was definitely a party happening now. The rooms had achieved that density of noise and movement, too much happening to take in properly, things seen sidelong, discontinuous. Loud laughter or shouting occasionally broke like thunder. When all the servants were sent away—all walking out of the kitchen doors to wherever it was they slept—Henry expected things to go up a notch and they did. Daoud came in with a tray of stuff, razor blades and shining mirrors and white baggies and several cloudy bongs for those who liked to keep it mellow.

Henry said to Virginia, "Are you into this?"

"Sure. A little."

"I know, right? Why not take the escalator? Beats walking."

When his turn came, he dipped down for a thick, fortifying line. He held his nose, scrunched his eyes against the worm of sensation crawling in his sinuses. "Holy fuck," he said. "That stuff is like cut with like even stronger cocaine. Fuck."

"Thanks for the warning there."

He watched Virginia inhale a slimmer stripe of powder. She approached delicately her own inverted reflection, a cat peering into a pond.

"You do that very prettily," he said. "I just snorted like a pig."

Virginia turned to face him, wide-eyed, a comic expression of shock on her face. "Wooh. Ayah."

"You're great," he said. "I feel like you understand me."

"You're not too hard to understand."

"I know this so far has only been like a few days in the history of the world and whatever ..."

"Oh wow. We're going into this. You can stop talking. We can do something fun instead."

"Come to the bathroom with me. I've been already. The bathroom's great. I can tell you how scared I am."

"Sounds like a party."

"And maybe get a little sugar, a little what-what. You know what I'm saying."

"You're gross. Let's go."

In the quiet of the bathroom he could feel the stimulants in him, a buzzing vibration as he stood still. Virginia put her hands in his hair and kissed him. The taste of her mouth, alcohol and chemicals and talk. The smoke on her skin. He lost himself in it for a moment, holding her tight, disappearing.

She pushed her hands against his chest and leaned back to breathe for a moment. "I get it. You're pleased to see me."

"I am."

"And you're scared, you were saying."

"Fuck me, I'm scared."

"Of what? Apparently according to Marta we could all actually be executed for the drugs here but that's not going to happen."

"No. Of this film, this job I've got. It's happening like as soon as I go back. I don't wanna go back. Let's run away."

"Oh, balls. Is that all? You're good at acting. I've seen you do it. I need to pee. You can keep talking."

"It is a little distracting. I mean, I know it's my job and I can do it ..."

Virginia arranged herself on the toilet, hunched forward and stared at a point on the floor to initiate her flow.

"But maybe I can't do it. And I've got to immediately stop eating again. I was starting to relax."

"Hey," she said, standing up and dropping her skirt. "You want me to show you an old model's trick?" She flushed and rinsed her hands. "An old ballet trick? That was what I wanted to do, by the way, when you asked me the other day. I was a dancer. Thought I was shit hot until I left Kentucky and found I wasn't even close. So this is the trick."

Henry felt an intriguing sensation of things warping, of the world gone mad, when she plucked a tissue from a gold box by the sink and pushed it into her mouth. "Little water," she said, muffled, and scooped some water from the tap. She closed her eyes, moved the thing around with her tongue, and swallowed. She showed him her empty mouth. "See. Few of those. You feel full for a long time. Then it goes right through you."

"I wanna try."

"Come to momma. Let's feed yer up."

The tissue had a neutral, pharmaceutical flavour. He folded it into his mouth, sipped water from the tap. Virginia encouraged him. With some strain, he manoeuvred it around and swallowed. He felt it travelling down. "See, it's not so hard?" she said. A communion of nothingness. "Delicious," he said. "Tissues are going to be my number one food group. Now how about that sugar?"

"Oh that. You still want that."

He came while somebody was knocking on the door. They emerged as one of the signifiers of a good party—the couple who leave the bathroom together after a suspiciously long time.

"Drink? Drugs?" he said. "Another line? Let's do another line."

Henry developed a theory that he explained to Virginia. It was about acting and film and how a film was a finished thing, sealed, the time inside it over. You're watching the past happening in the present. It's another dimension. Like where dead people are. That's where he wanted to be, where the dead people are.

"This is the most cokey coke talk I've heard for a long time. You should write this down. You'll enjoy it in the morning."

"There are like Thai women arriving. Are you seeing this?"

"I am. Well, my sisters must not be putting out. They've called the professionals."

"That is what it is, isn't it? That is kind of gnarly. We're in the gnarly stage of the party. Shall we go somewhere?"

"Where can we go?"

"Into the desert. I want to go into the desert. I'll ask that guy, Littlehampton or whatever he was called. We'll go out for a drive. This is a very good idea."

Henry climbed over the back of the sofa. "There he is. Hey, you, sir!"

Ilham agreed. "If you haven't been out there, you've got to see it."

*

Henry wound down his window to let the air stream in. He turned to Virginia, holding her hair flat against her head to stop it whipping around. "I have to go tomorrow," he said.

"I know."

"I like you."

"You don't have to."

"I know."

"Don't worry that you're tearing me apart here. I know what's going on. A three-day vacation."

"That kiss on the cheek? I didn't mean that."

"Just enjoy yourself."

"I will miss you," he said, and, though he was pretty sure he didn't mean it, he did feel it. For the moment he was sad, although another thought started to twist and change that emotion: in a few days he would be meeting Sofie Hadermann.

Ilham turned off the road. The car moved over desert surface, launching and sinking, launching and sinking.

"Woooh!" Henry gripped the handle in his door. Virginia hung on to his arm.

"Okay," Ilham shouted. "This is far enough." He switched the car off. They smiled at each other as they plunged into silence. "Go out and have a look," Ilham said.

They climbed out of the car into the dark moonscape. "What planet are we on?" Henry said.

"A fucked-up old bit of earth," Virginia said.

"Look up," Ilham said. "That's why you come out here."

"Oh my God," Henry said. "Virginia, are you seeing this?"

"Lots of stars," she said.

"Like so many. I've never seen them like this," Henry said.

"Grew up with them," she said. "Haven't seen 'em for a while."

"I need to … I'm sorry …" He wandered off on his own, looking upwards, stumbling softly until he felt he was alone. He fell down backwards onto the cold grip of the ground and looked up at the packed lights in the sky. He could see the long luminous cloud of the Milky Way, the whole entire galaxy he lived in, stars so many and so far that they were a veil of light. He could see stars behind stars. He'd never seen the night sky look three-dimensional before. There all the time. All the time. There all the time behind everything. Lying still, intoxicated, he felt the earth sway, the surface of the earth moving. The stars slid in his vision. He had to keep looking back at a certain point to reset them. The brilliant white fires. The endless space. It was awesome. His mind quailed. He was tired and sad and exhilarated. He felt a kind of exaltation in which happiness and despair were indistinguishable. Clichéd thoughts arrived—how big the universe is, how tiny he was, how alone—were unavoidable. Tiny and struggling. How nice it would be not to have to try, not to be a person, not to be himself at all.

Virginia called for him. "Hey, you! Where'd you go? We're waiting for you."

2

Flight

It was time to go. The number of her boarding gate had appeared when the screen refreshed. There it was. Kristin started walking, following the signs. It was easy to do, clear and flowing. She fell in with others walking, a movement of people so patterned that with a little swiftness, a little joy, it would be dancing. An electric vehicle beeped and carried past an infirm person wearing huge glasses and a baseball cap. Kristin hadn't been in an airport for a long time but many of her dreams were set in airports—in this very one—and part of her lived always here with the miracle happening, or about to happen, or failing to happen, while travellers blurred around her and she could somehow feel with heightened senses the heavy machinery of flight arched overhead.

The miracle had happened in this very airport and now she was back inside it, back inside the central magic of her life, on her way to see Henry again. She had visited the spot where it had happened earlier, where the watches glittered behind glass. The watches appeared in some of the dreams, too: she would hear them, chirruping, intelligent, their bright faces attentive to the moment, eternity come to see.

Moving walkways bore her forwards. They bounced underfoot. She held her coffee cup, her backpack on her shoulders. Soon she was at the gate, one of the first there, and she found a good seat facing the desk. She took out her phone and texted Suzanne. *In the airport. All good. Waiting to fly! xx.*

Through the enormous window, Kristin could see what must be the plane she would be getting on, tethered to its tunnel. Above, there were golden clouds. Kristin became engrossed in one, the silence of its slow, pouring transformations, stretching and gathering, flaring at the top into wisps that vanished. So much beauty if you only looked. Around her the few people in their chairs, dressed in soft leisurewear for the long-haul flight, didn't see. They looked instead at their phones, at books, at the floor.

Two years ago, after Ron had initiated the divorce and they were no longer living together, Kristin had come to this airport to fly down to the islands with Suzanne and Linda. The plan was for the vacation to be defiantly celebratory, drunk and outrageous. Kristin had been the first to arrive. She went to the check-in desk. She opened her bag for her passport and printed booking confirmation and had also found Spiderman. This had all come back to her entire when she went to the restroom in the airport earlier. Everything that had been broken into unconvincing pieces with strenuous recollection and partial reappearances in dreams had come together again. They still had the same brand of soap in the airport bathroom, a soft-serve of scented foam deposited automatically in your palm when you triggered the sensor. When Kristin had smelled it again earlier she had remembered standing there in tears, cooling her face with water, washing her hands. The ordinary, anonymous, chemical pleasantness of the soap's fragrance, mass-produced, made her yearn to be like that, to be as okay as everybody else in the crowds of passengers. It was the sight of Spiderman that had broken her. When she saw him in her bag, the tensed posture, the painted featureless face and white diamond eyes, she had known immediately that Lionel had put it in there because he wanted her to have it, his precious favourite toy, because he felt sorry for her and worried that she might be lonely.

And then with her eye makeup reapplied, her breath once more slow and regular, looking more or less normal, she had emerged from the restroom and met the actor Henry Banks and ordinary had been forbidden her forever.

Dazed, not quite able to identify the familiar face, she said, "Don't I know you?"

Henry smiled at her. He said, "You tell me. It seems like you do."

They had a brief conversation standing there in front of the display window of expensive watches and everything became very clear, overwhelmingly clear. When she met Suzanne and Linda later on, they were worried about her because she was so quiet and strange, flexing the fingers of her right hand and unable to tell them what had happened. There weren't words for it. A pure white circle of truth, a pure heat, now sat in the centre of her heart and flowed out, containing everything. A total sympathy. An end to questions. The nature of love. How could she speak about that?

Henry had shaken her hand. For a long time after it seemed singled out from the rest of her body. She would look at it, move it, as though it could if it wanted to share its special knowledge of him and tell her what would happen next.

And this was all because little Lionel had put his Spiderman toy in her bag. This was how you knew it was fate: the smallest thing different in either of their lives up to that instant and it wouldn't have happened. A traffic light's delay of half a minute and they would have used the airport independently, without ever seeing one another. If Lion hadn't put Spiderman in her bag she wouldn't have cried, she wouldn't have run to the restroom. If she hadn't opened her bag in that way she wouldn't have seen it. Fate. Seemingly so fragile but it rules like iron because it is meant to be.

The seats around Kristin were full now, all the people bound for London. She heard English voices behind her, a couple talking with the flat tang of one of those accents. Opposite, a young man in square glasses, wearing cargo pants and a mountaineering sweater, was reading the Bible. He had one of those beards trimmed to a line along his jawbone to mark the boundary between fat cheeks and a fat neck. A gate of goatee around his mouth. He turned a page. That was nice to see: a serious, spiritual person. He looked up and she smiled at him. He turned away, pensive, as though she were a question he now had to consider. Maybe she'd scared him. She hadn't meant to. Looking around, Kristin felt affection for all of the people travelling on this adventure together, forming into a group as the sky darkened outside—now an awesome vista of bronze and purple, a resonant and auspicious sky affirming the significance of the journey.

The journey had to be made. Kristin had known this for some time. She had long ago accepted that her letters to Henry would go unanswered and that she would have to go to him in person. When *Hamlet* first appeared in her Google alerts, she knew when it would be. And then, months later, when an alert pinged through a tiny article that said Henry's father had written a play (what a family!)

and had him boasting that his famous son would be at the premiere, just after *Hamlet*, the invitation couldn't have been more obvious if it had begun, *Kristin, come quickly*. She cancelled her ticket for *Hamlet* and at serious expense bought one for the last night from someone else. The first ticket she'd bought from the theatre, waking at three a.m. to be online and ready for four when the London box office would switch on. So prepared and yet the frantic inaccuracy of her typing when the moment came. The sense of victory at securing a ticket. Afterwards, she couldn't get back to sleep until after ten in the morning.

Two tones on the PA system like a doorbell, then a nasal British woman's voice. Kristin looked at the desk. The woman wore the airline's uniform's red neck scarf and had blond hair that spiralled into a bun high at the back of her head. She called the first category of passengers to board.

Kristin belted herself into her seat. She didn't have her coffee cup anymore. She must have left it on the floor outside. She had her book and her iPad now tucked into the seat pocket with the airline magazine and other things they gave you. Her backpack she'd pushed under the seat in front. Beside her, a small boy played with the straps of his belt while his mother, in the next seat along, told him to buckle it. Dressed in pyjamas and socks, he already had the pale, dignified, quietly observant look that children sometimes have after their bedtime. Lion did it, too, holding himself very erect and decent until he crumpled. The boy's soft flannel collar looked appealingly comfy against his delicate neck. The mother said, "No, do it now. The flight attendant will come and check that you've buckled in." The boy did now as he was told, his little striped feet kicking. Kristin said to him, "Hey, neighbour. Do you want to see what I've got in my bag?" She bent over to retrieve her backpack and smiled past the boy at the mother as she produced Spiderman.

"You always have that in your bag?" the mother asked.

"Oh, I guess I do. My stepson gave it to me." The boy was handling Spiderman now, checking the range of movement in his tensed limbs.

"I see. They're not travelling with you, your family?"

Kristin shook her head. No. They're … Well, to get into it, we got divorced a while back there. You know. Life."

"I see."

"It happens."

"So, your stepson? You see him? Is that what you call him, after a divorce, I mean?"

The boy bounced Spiderman's pointed red feet along his armrest.

"I don't know. I haven't really thought about that, to be honest. It's how I think of him."

What she thought of in that moment for no particular reason was Lion standing on the deck by the pond at Ron's house, chewing the edge of the towel he'd wrapped around himself, staring over the water.

"You see him ever?"

"Gosh. This is a lot of questions. Actually, there are three boys. The youngest gave me this. Why are you going to London?"

"My husband is there for a work thing. Thought we'd add on a vacation. You?"

"Similar. Same." Kristin said. "My life didn't stop with the divorce."

Flight attendants walked down the aisles banging shut the overhead lockers. On the small screens in front of them, a video of safety instructions played showing correct postures and procedures should the aircraft crash into the ocean. Kristin said, "In the past I've been a bit scared of flying but not today. Let's get up there."

The plane taxied, turned. Squares of orange light, the setting sun coming in through the windows, flowed over people's faces and slid along the walls. A loose roar like a big gas flame being lit, then a shuddering went through the seats and plastic fittings and the plane punched forwards, rumbling, picking up speed, lifting at the front, floating up from the ground. Small domestic lights could be seen in the countryside below.

After a meal, eaten while watching a postcard-sized movie with headphones on, most of Kristin's fellow passengers went to sleep, reclining under blankets. The little boy next to her passed out completely, limp as a doll. When the mother went off to the toilet, Kristin retrieved Spiderman from beside the boy's thigh and put him back in her backpack.

Even when the lights were dimmed to a soothing, nocturnal blue, even with her eyes closed and the blanket up to her chin, Kristin could not lose consciousness. She drifted in the swirl of her thoughts. The future was so close at hand its light was breaking through, too bright for sleep. Soon she would be seeing Henry live in the theatre. Soon she would be meeting him again at his father's play. Soon all that had been so long delayed would arrive. She smiled, her eyes still closed, images of smiles in her mind: Henry smiling, she herself smiling. From time to time she thought, I'm falling asleep now, and with that woke up. Maybe she did drop off at one point because an hour or so seemed to go missing. Also, the way an isolated memory returned to her suggested she was unconscious either side. The boy had kicked Kristin and she looked across at him being soothed and rearranged by his mother. He moaned at her with his eyes closed, at the mother who was always there outside his sleep.

They were flying east into the sunrise and the coming day and perhaps that had something to do with her wakefulness. When the flight attendant walked along the aisles opening all the window blinds, the daylight was shocking and brilliant. As the plane tilted, Kristin could see below a blazing platform of cloud. The plane sank into it slowly, whiteness whipping past the windows. Beneath, the earth was in view with quietened colours. Vegetable greens and browns of small fields. Britain, just as everyone said it would be. After rapid miles, London was below them for a long time. And then more fields and finally the lowered wheels banged onto the runway.

"We're here," Kristin said. "We're here."

People turned their phones back on. Kristin did too and texted Suzanne. *Landed in London. It's happening!* Around her, people sprang upright to retrieve their hand luggage then stood grimacing while they waited for the doors to open.

What a boring effort it was getting through the airport. The corridors at Heathrow were so long and passport control was an age of slowly advancing, waiting again, slowly advancing.

At the baggage carousel, Kristin watched the other passengers waiting for their possessions to reappear, eager to disperse. The forced passivity of the flight over, their faces hardened again into individuality, a sense of the importance of their own lives. When their suitcases appeared, they took them and left at speed. When hers came bumping around, Kristin did the same.

Kristin had decided to take the London Underground to the hotel. The tube was a famous sight in itself so her tour of the city would begin immediately. She bought a ticket, made her way through the snapping jaws of the barrier and descended. Tiles. Posters. A tang in the air of singed electrical metal and dirt. A few people, also with suitcases, were already waiting on the platform. The train banged out of the tunnel and rushed to a stop in front of her. The doors opened. Inside, there was no obvious place for a suitcase. Kristin sat down and held hers in front of her knees. A warning sound and the doors closed. The train moved on to the next station and opened its doors to different, non-airport passengers. They were dressed for work, faces soft with fatigue, unfocused, but ready to endure, almost all of Indian ethnicity. Kristin saw in them the effort of mornings, getting up, showering, dressing, eating, digesting, moving, beginning. Life was so hard for people. After a few more stops, the train rattled up from underground into daylight, a sudden sideways morning light that pushed against Kristin's tired brain. Kristin saw the brick backs of houses, their toothy TV aerials and satellite dishes, bits of roads and traffic, an ordinary, altered world with different street signs, smaller cars. Again the train sank into darkness.

The carriage was very full now. Kristin wished she could make her suitcase disappear as people packed around it, holding the overhead bar and acting like she and her case weren't there, reading their phones and papers, listening to headphones, disseminating a general dislike from their stiff, stoical postures. Arriving at her stop, Kristin had to get up somehow and push her way out. She did so, crushing herself through and out onto the platform. After the other passengers had streamed past her she felt her heart surge with panic when she saw that she was almost eye to eye with Henry. He was in a poster—she knew the image already very well from the internet—his face slashed with shadows, a skull in his hand. You couldn't say that it was a sign, exactly, given that she was there to see his final performance and of course it would be advertised, but still it felt like something, like the click of synchronization, like all the little gears in the watches in the airport were whirring for a reason, ticking, ticking. Looking into Henry's familiar face, Kristin's panic gave way, its heat flowering outwards as a great serenity. Kristin had grown used to such sensations after meeting Henry—itching hands, a burning in her chest that could wake her in the night, thick waves of sexual desire, a bright spinning in the pit of her stomach. This was all part of the revelation of Henry and the nature of love. A whole new body had been revealed, feverishly radiant and spiritual, connecting beyond her own limits to the whole universe.

Vast escalators carried Kristin back up to the surface of the world. She exited onto a loud street at Holborn and looked around to see that she stood at the bottom of grand buildings. The architecture was serious and historical, a bit like parts of old Philly only better. It was Britain as Kristin expected it to be, a storybook enchantment, but cut through with rapid traffic and shops. Kristin found the map to her hotel on her phone.

The Windsor Hotel was in a narrow house on a long street of repeating buildings along which large trees with pale, peeling trunks at intervals filtered the light. They were in leaf, the tender green translucency of spring. The season was further advanced than it was back home. Not only had the flight thrust her into the next day, it had carried Kristin further into the future, her future. At the reception desk, Kristin was given her key card, the door codes, the wifi password, the breakfast hours, and directed upstairs. The room was tiny with a tinier bathroom attached.

There was a wardrobe, a single bed with a textured green coverlet, a bedside table with a digital clock and a half-size kettle with cups and sachets of drinks. A window looked into a bricked inner space with pipework and other windows in which trapped sounds of voices and traffic softly diminished. This was not a room that Ron would have put up with for one moment, even with its excellent location. But for Kristin it was ideal, a little London nest to rest in. Ron had a scrupulous eye for faults in hotel rooms and restaurants, for customer service that was less than eager. He would complain, authoritatively, and waited for discounts and compensation that he always got. It was a striking early lesson for Kristin in how rich people did things, how negotiable high prices actually were.

Kristin unpacked. She balanced her toiletries on the rim of the bathroom sink. She placed her wadded clothes on the shelves of the wardrobe and hung up blouses and skirts. At the bottom of her suitcase her dress lay folded. She put her fingers into the sleeves and lifted it up. Barely a crease. Midnight blue. The cut was kind of fifties, demure but flirtatious, with a flattering broad band around the waist and a skirt that kicked out just below the knee. When she had had bangs cut into her dark hair, two different people had told Kristin that she looked like Zooey Deschanel.

Kristin lay on the textured bedcover to rest, maybe sleep for an hour. Her eyelids were hot and fragile; they trembled as though they couldn't stay closed. She felt warm and unclean in the clothes she'd travelled in for hours, halfway across the world. She decided to take a shower. She really was tired: it was an effort to lift the weight of her limbs up from the bed.

The water pressure was good but the cubicle was confiningly small and the shower head shot out a narrow diameter of water so that she had to keep moving, bumping into the plastic walls, and sweeping the water over her body with her hands. She had depilated thoroughly in preparation for the trip. Her hands slipped easily over the smooth shapes of her hairless flesh. Dry again, she put on the short white robe provided by the hotel and once more lay down on the bed.

Kristin woke up feeling cold in a small hotel room in a foreign country, unsure of the time, daylight flaring around the curtains over a small window. Somehow, she had become unplugged from her fate. She lay disconnected and as she remembered everything, she thought herself a fool, a fantasist. She had travelled all this distance, spent all this money, for no good reason. Kristin had decided this many times in the past. Sometimes, she found relief in the thought. The burden of having to act, to undergo this humiliation on behalf of the future was lifted from her and the ordinary, spacious, uninteresting freedoms were restored. But immediately the other inextinguishable thought returned. It did now. It would never leave her. Some things just are, inescapably true. You don't even know how you know. Her fate was inexorable and wonderful. She would have to meet it whatever she did. Kristin slid her legs off the edge of the bed and stood up. There was the day to get through before the night that would lead on to tomorrow and her first encounter.

Outside, London continued about its business, adding another busy day to its long history. Kristin picked her way through the pedestrians and found a nearby Pret A Manger sandwich place to eat in. She liked these places, the brushed metal surfaces and music, the reliable quality of the food. She often went in Philly and she felt a little ashamed to immediately resort to these home comforts here. Later, when she was more awake, she would look for authentic British food. She took her choices from the chiller cabinets over to the baseball-capped staff behind the counter. She paid a surprising amount of money—cartoonishly bright coloured paper money—for a sandwich lush with mayonnaise, a small juice and a packet of raisins coated in sickly hardened yogurt. Around her as she ate she heard through the music snatches of the conversation of two women in business suits sitting at the next table. They were trying to identify someone in an anecdote. Tall? No. With the trendy glasses? That'll be him. Through the windows, Kristin watched people passing, the traffic of cars and buses and taxis, the indescribable strangeness of London that was so near at hand.

She wiped the corners of her mouth with a stiff paper napkin. What should she do to fill her time? She had her list of things to see. The Houses of Parliament. Buckingham Palace. The butterfly exhibit at the Natural History Museum—that she would go and see with Henry, a trip she'd planned since she read about the live butterflies you could walk through. Trafalgar Square. The British Museum was nearby. She could go there.

Somehow the place was hard to locate although wide, grand and obvious once found. After airport-style security where her bag was checked and she passed through the empty doorway of a metal detector, Kristin entered the museum. She discovered a huge white space of light and geometry and a surf of voices. In its centre was another closed building. This wasn't what she was expecting. She'd pictured wood and brass and history. There were shops in this area and information desks and chunks of ancient sculpture staring blindly about. The size of the place, the movement of the crowd reminded Kristin of her travelling and made her feel tired. There was a coffee shop over on the right, hissing and clattering, and she headed for caffeine. More queuing, more money and Kristin had a coffee. She took it to a table and sat. A school party walked past, two teachers and a group of chest-high children, maybe nine or ten years old, in blue pants and sweaters. A few of the girls had their heads tightly wrapped in Muslim headscarves.

Kristin sipped her coffee. An old couple sat down at the table with a tray of tea and cakes. They separated out their cups and plates. Having smiled at Kristin, they then stopped still and seemed to be taking a moment to recover, like swimmers just out of rough water. They breathed. They rested their eyes on near things, the tray, their hands, the tabletop.

"Hi," Kristin said. "How are you? I've never been here before. It's so big."

"Oh," the woman said. She seemed surprised to be spoken to. "Is that right?"

"It is. My first time in London. I might be spending a lot of time here in the future."

"I see. We don't come that often. We're from Bedford, aren't we?" The man nodded, confirming. "You don't know where that is, I expect."

"I don't."

"We come for the big exhibitions but it wasn't all that and the tickets even with the discount are a lot."

"I thought the museum was free."

"Not for the Vikings."

"What should I see?"

"What should she see? Egyptians are the main thing. Mummies. Greek sculptures as well. I mean, there's plenty to keep you busy."

"The mummies it is, then. You have a wonderful day."

"Just looking forward to getting home again."

A crowd shifted around the glass cases with their phones out, taking photos. Large labels explained the Egyptian gods, the bird-headed god, the dog-headed god, the dynasties, the soul sitting in the celestial scales, their whole alien world, hard and gold with bright painted eyes. Kristin read and looked at illustrations as she waited to get closer. Stopped figures among rushes, maps of the Nile delta, ancient names as weird as those down in Mexico. She knew about ancient Egypt, of course. Everyone did. It was standard museum stuff, famous world history, like the Eiffel Tower and dinosaurs and Michelangelo's *David* and wooden battleships. But she'd never stopped to look at them, to look at actual real Egyptian things. What had they known, these people? What had been lost? How could all these glittering, elaborate, wise things have just fallen out of the world? Mysteries had been lost.

Kristin arrived at a body in a painted sarcophagus. The person in the coffin was small, dry, an autumnal brown colour, modest, bandaged, just a little dead guy who had no idea what was going on around him. She wanted to help him understand. He looked so lonely. It was terrible. She felt sorry for him, sad at the sight of other tourists on the other side of the glass staring down. She wanted to be his friend. They could leave together, him with his peanut-head and noseless face and little mousey teeth, talking in his magical language of bleeps and chirps. She felt he had plenty to tell her and that she of all people would understand.

People pressed behind her. She had to leave the little pharaoh to his fate.

So many treasures, jars and gods and so many other things to see. Rooms and rooms of it. Kristin was too tired to absorb any more. She found her way back to the main hall where she bought a bookmark of Egyptian hiero-glyphs as a souvenir. She should get things for Suzanne's kids at some point but she couldn't think about it now.

On her way back to the hotel she bought a salad in a plastic box to eat in her room.

Just one more night, one more sleep, and she would be seeing Henry again in the flesh.

She fell asleep easily, heavily, her mind replaying remembered motion of trains and planes and blurry streets. She awoke in darkness and saw the unlikely digits 3:33 on the bedside clock. They shed faint green light onto the table's surface. There was a red light on the wall, the TV on standby. There was a dingy orange light behind the curtains. There were voices some-where, a drunken argument or celebration, she couldn't tell. Perhaps they had woken her up. Certainly she was now sharply awake. The voices faded. She heard the sound of some metal object, a can probably, bouncing on a sidewalk. The voices were gone.

Unused to a single bed, Kristin kept turning and coming to its edge, the verge of falling. She stopped moving and impersonated perfect relaxation as a way to fall asleep again, lying completely still on her side, serene on the pillow, her knees bent, her hands palm to palm beside her face. She was hungry but ignored the feeling. She kept her eyes closed like she was hiding in a game and counting to a hundred. She waited.

*

The alarm, persisting, broke apart Kristin's nonsensi-cal dream about a plumbing problem of blockages and awful, humiliating smells and Suzanne on the phone to

134

their mother and contractors filling her empty house. Everything was fine, naturally, as Kristin heard busy morning noises and saw her hotel room again, but a sense of sordid disrepair and disorder lingered like a judgment.

Kristin had set her alarm for the hotel breakfast and she quickly dressed and went downstairs, following the signs for the dining room. She hardly needed to check the signs: the warm, animal smell of frying would have guided her there. She stood obediently by the instruction to wait to be seated. The room was small, cozy, swarming with pattern on carpets and curtains. Only one table was currently occupied: a middle-aged couple, the man lean, chewing, the woman round-shouldered with grey-blond hair, her back to Kristin. They looked foreign somehow, like their mouths would not produce English when they spoke.

A waitress appeared. She did speak English but with a European accent. "Good morning. You are room?"

"My room? I'm in twenty-two." A flash of memory: the clock showing 3:33. Who knew what that meant?

"Okay." The waitress made a note in a ledger. Kristin thought she might be a student, that she wasn't serious in her role of being a waitress. Perhaps it was the way her outfit didn't quite fit. Her black polyester skirt ballooned at her waist. "Please. Where you like." She gestured at the room.

Kristin sat down at a circular table. The couple said something to each other. German, maybe.

The waitress handed Kristin a menu card. "Tea? Coffee? Orange juice? Apple?"

"Coffee, yes, and orange, please."

The waitress walked away, looking at her pad.

In the tinkling silence of plates and flatware, Kristin felt awkward. She called across to the other table, "Good morning."

"Good morning to you," the man answered. His wife turned around and smiled. "Good morning," she said. Her voice shocked Kristin, a smoker's voice, deep and rasping. It was as though she had revealed a deformity. The man had a bland face, square, narrow-lipped, without emphasis. He looked like someone who did a technical job, Kristin thought, some kind of engineer, or one of the chemists Ron used to work with. That thought put Kristin off. She said no more and the silence was resumed.

*

After all the hours, all the days, the letters, she was there. How had the day gone? Didn't matter. It had gone. After breakfast, she'd returned to her room to digest. More sleep and waking and fear as large things moved into place. She'd gone out for a walk with no purpose, an elongation of streets and people and trees and pigeons. She'd gone back, eaten a sandwich, rested, slowly dressed and finally left. Down into the racketing yellow violence of the underground trains and up among glassy buildings and now here she was at the Barbican, a multi-storey arts centre like a shopping mall or a car park or a government building. On grim grey walls Henry's face appeared beside other pictures, one of a ballet dancer posed inside a floating ribbon, the other a gasping, gesticulating conductor with flying hair.

Kristin found her way to the cloakroom and handed over her coat. She wore a dark blue cardigan over her dress. She walked, holding the strap of her handbag. Henry would not appear out here in the audience area but he was somewhere in this building.

136

Kristin was early. She bought a small, expensive pot of nuts from a bar and sat on a black leather bench eating them one by one, feeling squirrely and very alert.

She bought the program for *Hamlet*. She also picked up every flyer from one of the information stands. She didn't know why. She piled them beside her on another seat while she peered at the familiar rehearsal photos in the program.

A bell sounded. The Barbican theatre was now open for this evening's final performance of *Hamlet*. Kristin went in immediately, leaving the flyers behind on the seat. As she approached the young girl in a black uniform checking tickets, Kristin felt a rush of fear that there would be a problem and she'd be refused but of course this did not happen, and Kristin was told fourth door on the left and the girl held out her hand to the next customer behind her.

There were two actors on the stage, dressed in modern military uniforms, already acting, pacing up and down between poles with CCTV cameras mounted on them, staring out towards the audience. The seats around Kristin started to fill. Bells for five minutes, three minutes, one minute. Kristin twisted around to see all the people behind her and above on the sloping shelves of the upper levels. Two ushers appeared at the doors on either side of the auditorium, walking up and down the outside steps, checking, waiting, whispering into walkie-talkies. Simultaneously on some cue, mechanically synchronized, all the doors shut, sealing everybody inside. Music started, a few ominous notes, and a sound effect of the distant sea. The first words were spoken by the two soldiers, quick and nervous, and after a minute or so another character appeared there on stage, standing in a long coat in the gloom. It wasn't Henry. A ghost appeared, flickering in CCTV images on a screen behind them. In the next scene the lights were bright, everybody wore smart suits or evening dresses, and Henry was right there, clearly visible. His suit and tie were black. He looked miserable. He said nothing for the longest time. Kristin felt the curved air of the transparency between them, the space from her seat to the stage. She could get up and walk to him. She could call out and he would hear her. His voice was in her ears. He spoke so much, so loudly, sometimes small and close and quiet, alone on the stage, controlling everyone in the room. When he touched the two women on stage, the tiny girl playing Ophelia, the rich-voiced, disdainful actress playing his mother, Kristin was held by a brief, numb arrest, not quite understanding the graphic, intimate irrelevance of it. (She had researched these women online some time ago, Lucy and Alexandra; she knew their marital statuses; she wasn't worried.) Kristin resented the intermission, being driven out of her seat and into the trivial chatter and snacks and driven back in again, returned to the solidity of her seat. The events of the play got worse and worse, as she knew they did. Soon Henry had that skull in his hand, just as he did in the poster. Every image of Henry that Kristin had ever seen, every moment of *The Grange* and everything else that she'd found, was of this living man who she knew, moving in front of her. It wasn't long before, in a glitter of sword blades clashing and cutting the air, Henry was dying, then dead. A horrifying sight. A few more words and it was over. It was such a relief to applaud, the final silence of the play collapsing under a wave of noise from the audience. There were whistles and cries.

People rose to their feet. Kristin did. The actors came back onto the stage in sequence, Henry last of all, himself again, happy, grateful, jogging down to the front to bow. There were cheers. Kristin whooped. Henry held his hands to his heart and bowed again. He retreated, taking the hands of the actors beside him and the long line of them bowed together. They repeated this then left, the last two actors to clear the stage chatting inaudibly to each other, evidently themselves once more.

Kristin was so happy and light as she left with everybody else. She hardly noticed the others around her—she was preoccupied with all that she'd seen, gathering it inside herself. She was almost out of the door of the building when she remembered her coat in the cloakroom and went back.

*

They were onstage together. Strong lights angled down from overhead. Kristin could feel the heat of them on her skin. Sometimes they swept through her field of vision like headlights or stars. Darkness was wrapped around them. In its outer reaches, it prickled with the unseen eyes of spectators. Henry was upset, frantic, as he had been in the play. He was pale and couldn't focus. Kristin was trying to help him. Other characters appeared for short scenes of anxious, incomprehensible communication. A soft, smiling man held a dagger then became irrelevant somehow. Kristin took hold of Henry's forearm to steady him. He was grateful, relieved, as if she'd saved him from drowning. They stood closer together in a turning column of light. He was so near, Kristin wanted so desperately to kiss him that she strained to

139

close the final distance, pushing her face across the fabric of her pillow, her lips parting, her eyes opening.

*

The Germans were there already, in the same places as yesterday. Kristin greeted them. "Good morning. How are you today?"

"You look well." The man smiled and his wife turned around quickly, unsmiling, to see. From this, Kristin knew that the man was flirting with her, that he did it often, that his wife hated it.

"I'm good," she said, as though he'd asked her a question. She walked to her table.

"The weather is improved," the man pursued. "The sun is out today."

This was true. Kristin looked up and saw a bridal whiteness in the net curtains. The patterned carpet at Kristin's feet glowed. The universe was happy for her, sharing in her secret. The Germans felt very far away while Kristin ordered poached eggs on wholemeal from the waitress and took out her phone.

A voicemail message. Her mother. Despite the expense, despite the annoyance she knew she would feel, she pressed the button to listen, just in case it was something worse than the usual.

I just heard from Suzy you're in England going after that actor you met that one time. Well, Krissy, I've made myself clear as I can on that subject some time ago without any effect as I can see. I just hope you're being careful over there. Look, I'm not saying ...

Kristin took the phone from her ear and hit three to delete. Usually, her mother's anger—a permanent state since Kristin "lost" Ron—was expressed as a quiet, general pessimism, a softly spreading stain of complete disillusion with Kristin at its centre. She never said a word. From this there was no escape. Now the attack was direct and could be ignored. Her mother knew nothing of life, really. A few years ago, she had seen a local news report about a woman who was making a fortune from collectibles on eBay and she had decided to do the same. Now there was a closet in her room—which she treated like a huge secret though she told everyone about her hobby—stacked with Disney Princess dolls pristine in their plastic packaging. Rainbows and snowflakes and zooming stars decorated the boxes. The dolls smiled emptily through the cellophane window. This was the image that came to mind when Kristin remembered her mother's useless opposition. Those dolls should be played with, alive in the magic of some little girl's game.

*

Kristin had expected more from Buckingham Palace. Broad, blank, set back behind its black gates, it had nothing of the castle about it, no towers or turrets. The gleaming, dull-eyed guardsmen, polished and creaseless, with shining weapons and standing absolutely still were the most interesting thing there. Tourists moved around them, stood beside them and in front of them, leaning in with their phones on selfie sticks and the guards didn't flinch. Kristin took out her own phone and took a few pictures of the building and a guard. She took a selfie, too, turning her back to Buckingham Palace and arranging it over her shoulder, dipping her forehead and lifting her gaze. Something to post on Facebook or send to Suzanne or her mother. As she was putting her phone back in her pocket an American voice asked, "Hi there. Would you mind taking a picture for us?" Kristin turned. A small woman in a blue fleece with short grey hair combed down evenly in all directions. Her silent husband, smiling, was exactly the same height as she was and that made them look a little silly, Kristin thought, when she took their camera. She kept her voice quiet and her accent unidentifiable when she said "okay" and the couple shuffled together. "One, two, three." Their smiles grew fiercer. Kristin pressed the button. She handed the camera back. They thanked her as they checked the image and Kristin walked away, keen to avoid conversation and stay in her private thoughts where Henry was. She stopped to look up at Queen Victoria on her crowded monument, stern, pudgy, unattractive, her blank, bored eyes staring into the traffic.

There was a park. Kristin walked into it. That was better. Leaves and light. Choral arrangements of colourful flowers in flowerbeds. Squirrels bounded between trees, scampered up the sides of bins. A smell of life from the ground and soft grass. She sat down on a bench to wait out some more of this meaningless interval. It occurred to her that a butterfly should fly past through the spring air bearing its secret message for her. No butterfly came but, hey, it didn't matter. Everything was still faultlessly in place. Kristin thought of where to go next.

*

The escalator was silver and vast, like the side of a pyramid. It climbed towards white sky and delivered Kristin at a metallic arch. She passed through the ticket barriers and into a wide plaza. The wind was quick, a river wind, blowing across the width of the Thames. A different world, a whole different London. Kristin inhaled. The light was dazzling, the buildings sharp and modern. From interviews, Kristin knew that Henry lived in this neighbourhood. His eyes looked on these things, this sky, these walkways with their Sunday strollers, those white boats.

There were more people on the path by the river. Kristin stopped and leaned against a rail to look at the water. Where the sun struck there was a crater of glittering white light, pulsing with tiny movements, too bright to look at for long. Elsewhere the water was brown, swift, sombre, serious. The flowing movement was absorbing to watch. It gave Kristin a sensation of drifting, anchored to the rail but in motion. She turned her eyes towards the light and closed them, letting the wind fuss noisily around her head. When she opened her eyes again there was something in the water moving towards her, a dog, a dead dog, its jaws open, its face just under the surface, beneath the window of the water. Its front paws flopped in the current, loose. It slowly rotated. The fur looked dowdy, like worn carpet. Kristin turned to see if anyone else had seen it but no one was looking. This must happen now and again, Kristin reasoned, dogs falling into the water. There was nothing there to think about. It had crossed, gone past towards the sea in silence. So much for Suzanne's accusation that Kristin only ever saw what she wanted to see. She certainly hadn't wanted to see that. It stayed in her mind, the strange ugly peacefulness of it drifting and turning.

Kristin walked on, among the Sunday people. You could somehow feel it was Sunday, everyone moving in a lull of recovery, living their actual lives for a change, couples holding coffee cups and pushing strollers together. There was a hint here of something coming in Kristin's future, given that this was where Henry lived, of a large, placid, domestic peace that they would share, washed in the freshness of the river air. She could picture so easily how they would weave together in the little rituals, the wordless rhythm of good habits, dressing and undressing together, cooking, watching TV and snuggling up, the ordinary plentiful safe feeling of love in a life. She looked mildly around, diffusing her blessing over the scene, until she saw a man who looked like Henry bouncing through it, who was Henry, the back of Henry's head getting farther away as he ran. Adrenalin burned the breath out of her chest and stopped her. She struggled into her next step and hurried after him. Was it him? It did seem like him. She was sure it was him. He was turning a corner where the railings bent to the right. She had to run herself, to jog, her backpack thumping her shoulder. She turned and could still see him. She slowed, breathless, but kept going in long urgent strides. It was him, definitely. She was where he lived. It was all true. It was all coming together. Fate sometimes just smacks you upside the head. He turned again, off the main walkway. Kristin sprinted as fast as she could but he was gone when she got there. She heard a door close in one of the buildings and she could feel where he had been. She walked to the source of the sound and found that she was right. *Henry Banks* was printed on a small white label by one of the buzzers on the intercom. No special font or sign, like he was just another person. And he was inside. He was safe. Kristin, breathing hard, her bangs sticking to her moist forehead, could feel him in there. Should she press the button? She couldn't. It was too soon. She wasn't prepared, either mentally or in her outfit and appearance. Kristin looked at that small, magical name. How it crawled and twisted inside her heart! She knew that she should stick to the original plan. Everything was falling into place, just as it was meant to be. Everything was going to be all right. Perhaps she would deliver a letter there later. How wonderful now to have his home address and not have to send everything through his agent.

*

When she walked into the dining room, the German man was alone, looking at something on his phone through reading glasses, head tilted back, eyelids half lowered. His face looked severe, old, disappointed. But when he looked up and saw Kristin, it changed, almost convulsed into a smile. It wasn't pleasant to see. He pulled off his glasses with a quick movement.

"Good morning," he said.

"And to you."

"My wife packs," he said. "We leave later today."

"Well, I hope you had a good time."

"For sure."

He fell silent, returning his attention to his phone while Kristin ordered her breakfast. When she was done, he put his phone in his hip pocket, his glasses into his top pocket, and came over to Kristin's table.

"So, I will say goodbye now."

"Okay. Goodbye."

"Goodbye."

He bent down and kissed her on the cheeks, his hands on her shoulder blades to pull her into him, though she resisted and their chests did not make contact. He smiled down at her as though they together had stolen a quick, illicit pleasure. "Have a good stay," he said. Then he left and Kristin was alone.

Kristin remembered this feeling of being alone in a room after such an incident, left to sort it in her mind, to interpret, to ignore, to decide to forget. This happened frequently in the early days with Ron when she was his PA and working in his new home office. A friendly squeeze of her upper arm, a pat on her lower back, brushing some fleck from her jacket collar and adjusting her hair. Sometimes he would lean down beside her to read a document on her screen, one hand on the back of her chair, his face so close beside hers she could feel the blurred beginning of touch. She knew what Ron was doing and she made a choice she now regretted, a bad, materialistic choice. Those drives out from Philly to near Valley Forge, the large house in its trees. The times when Ron's wife went out and they were alone. Later, after the game had played out, and he told her that he wanted a divorce, she wanted to shout *No! This is all wrong! Don't tell me you don't love me! It was me. I was the one who didn't love you. Not for a moment.*

*

The tourist sites weren't nearly as interesting to Kristin as the places of Henry's London and there was one address lodged in her memory that Kristin decided to visit. She wanted to know what the office looked like, to see where this part of the drama of her life had played out. All those envelopes that she'd written out by hand and she'd never wondered what the office looked like. She had in her mind only a flash of generic glass partitions, desks, swiftly walking suits, ringing phones. Envelopes with butterflies on them, full with the reality of love, with many details of her life, had gone to an address that was in her mind like a melody. She looked it up using the hotel's wifi and went.

The street had a strange name, Stanhope Mews. The sight of it dispelled Kristin's weak preconceived images of a busy, wordly, Hollywood players kind of place, and replaced it with a much better reality. A mews turned out to be a kind of side street cul-de-sac. To enter this one you turned off a main street and found yourself in a small, cobbled, sloping, uneven row of buildings like something from Dickens, everything as soft and irregular and alive as in a painting. In front of one door was a barrel turned into a planter and spilling red geraniums into the sunlight. There were plants and flowers everywhere, in pots and boxes and hanging baskets by every door, in window boxes above. The English did love their gardens. Naturally her letters had flown to a place like this for their rendezvous with Henry Banks, this sweet and lyrical street. She walked down the smooth, small stones, checking the different doors and their signs. Some kind of branding company. An asset management company. Something that didn't explain what it was with *Dorian Inc.* on a brass plate. And there was Haverford and Styles, Henry's agency, number eleven Stanhope Mews, SW7, in the flesh. A quiet doorway beside a wide window. Kristin looked through the reflections on the panes to see into the room within. There was movement, a dim shape of someone's head. Kristin pulled back, picturing herself seen from the other side, framed, garish in daylight, peering in. She walked on up the mews as though looking for somewhere else, down to the front of the building that closed off the end. With no farther to go, she turned and walked back. Now there was someone outside Haverford and Styles, a woman sucking on a vape pen. Kristin slowed her pace. The woman released the button and sighed out a big cloud of steam or whatever was in those things. Her hair was cut in a bob; at the bottom, two sharp point swung forwards. Her black jacket matched her hair; it too was angularly cut in hanging panels. Smooth plastic jewellery bulged on her fingers. But her knees under wrinkled opaque tights conveyed a different mood. A vulnerable human being could be seen in those knees. They reassured Kristin. She said, "Hey."

The woman looked up. "Hello?" she asked.

"Hi," Kristin said.

"Can I help you? Are you looking for something?"

"No. Not really. I'm like a tourist I guess."

"I see."

Kristin stood and smiled while the woman put the vape pen back in her mouth, pressed the button and inhaled.

"Do you work here?" Kristin asked.

"Yes, I do."

"Wow."

"You're not an actress, are you? Because I have to tell you door-stepping agents is not going to get you ..."

"I'm not an actress. Don't worry." Kristin laughed. "My gosh, no. You work with some cool people here, I guess."

"I do. Is this ... I'm confused. How do you know what we do here?"

"Oh, I've sent a lot of letters here. You represent Henry Banks, don't you?"

"He's one of my clients. Are you?"

"What?"

"You write letters to Henry care of us?"

"I have done. Yes."

"A lot of letters. Really, a lot."

"Sure. I like to stay in touch. We met once and ..."

"You're Twice-A-Week, aren't you?

"Sorry. What?"

"You're American. You write a couple of times a week. I know who you are. We call you Twice-A-Week in the office."

"Okay. Wow, okay. So ..."

"Should I be worried that you're here? Just turning up like this?"

"I don't think so. Why would you be?"

*

He shouldn't have come. This was too public. He was out of the protected precincts. At the top of a flight of stairs in a building by Borough Market, he'd found a group of strangers waiting, hanging up bags, changing into loose trousers, some of them stretching straightened legs or, seated, pulling on a foot. When he entered, he was observed with quiet curiosity. In a few faces, this thickened to recognition but no one said anything. They turned away again. Henry had nothing to fear. Lucy had already assured him that it would be fine for him, that he'd get what he needed. Lucy, his Ophelia, was young, barely out of drama school and hardly known. She would blend in entirely here. Henry observed a couple of art school–type kids sitting together. Tiny, with precise, ornate hair and wistful tattoos, they wore oversized black t-shirts. One was untying a shoelace. They were examples of the new exquisite, gender-fluid people who made Henry feel heftily male and crude. Henry had a quick look at his phone. No message from Lucy and no sign of her in the room. She'd said she might not make it. Henry concluded he was alone. Lucy had told him to go to the introductory talk beforehand and Henry looked around for who it might be who would give it. Maybe he should have had someone come to his place instead. It might have been an easier, better experience: some authentic Tibetan guy. Henry was steeling himself to ask someone about the talk when a shaven-headed man, barefoot, entered the room. He wore a black robe that swished, making a little rush of air. He said, "If there are any new people, would you like to follow me?" This man looked around, smiling, his bare head and neck turning turtle-like from side to side. Henry raised his hand. A short woman in black leggings and a long t-shirt stepped forward also. "Great. Good. Okay then. Come along this way." The man spoke rapidly, forcefully. Henry fell in behind him as they went down a short corridor to an adjacent room. Whatever its usual purpose was—some kind of gym or dance studio?—it had now been arranged into a rectangle of rush mats and flat black cushions with a low wooden boundary at the near end. At the far end sat a Buddha on a small stand, a bell, an incense burner, a few flowers. By the door, meditation cushions were stacked ready for use.

"Right. So here you collect a cushion and any of the smaller cushions you might need for support, under your knees maybe if you aren't so flexible, and as you enter the space you bow like this." The robed man demonstrated, palms together, bending at the waist with a straight back, as though hinged in the middle. "Or like this, if you're holding a cushion, which you will be." He repeated the action with only one hand held up. He was rapid and eager. If he had recognized Henry, he gave no sign of it.

He led them into the meditation area and demonstrated how to sit with their hands in their laps, left hand over right, their thumb tips touching. He explained the correct angle of the head, that they should endure pain without moving until the bell rang, to allow any small discomfort simply to pass. Between rounds of meditation there would be walking, slow and conducted in a particular style. He pressed his hands down on the mat, swung his feet under him and was vertical to demonstrate. He sat back down. The point was, he explained, to relax and to focus. We are all of us in our everyday lives tired, distracted, busy. He did a physical impression of typing at a computer, hands wiggling under his chin, eyes half closed, mouth hanging open. "But here," he brightened, straightened, "we sit up and breathe and focus." Henry thought that the hook for an impression of this man was obvious, his rapid switching. When he was still, he crystallized. When he spoke or moved, he was completely active. He explained that they should stay focused on their breathing and allow their thoughts to pass. If they liked they could name them—planning, worrying, fantasizing—as a way of letting them go. "You can stay where you are, if you want," he said. "Just turn and face the wall. I will go and get the others in to start the session." Henry did as he was told. Outside the door, the man hit some kind of wooden block, a clean, bare sound, and Henry could hear the others coming in, could feel their steps on the floor. He thought he could feel the prickling of their attention on him, inspecting the vulnerable back of his head. Shapes in his peripheral vision were two people settling either side of him. No more bouncing of footsteps. The man in the robes seemed to be back, shifting about near the Buddha. He settled. There was a sharp whack of a small wooden block and then the mellow sound of a large bronze bell lingering away into silence. It had begun. They were meditating.

Henry thought his posture probably looked very good. He was pretty ripped at the moment. *Hamlet* had kept him fitter than the gym with all the sword-fighting that needed re-rehearsing endlessly for health and safety. The choreography was still all there in his mind. He could get up and go into it now. His head was nobly erect, his shoulders wide and square, his legs neatly crossed beneath him, his hands serenely folded in his lap. Chap in robes could presumably see him and see what a natural he was. He did as he'd been told and attended to his breath, the narrow streams of air flowing in and out of his nostrils. A discomfort in his hips, a muscle on the right side gripping tighter and tighter, he resolved with a small adjustment in the angle of his spine. A few millimetres towards the right and the muscle let go; his weight dropped straight down through his buttocks into the floor. See, he was good at this. He had landed. That was the sensation he was after, to rest on the ground, earthed. How much time had passed? Probably only a few minutes. There were noises from the street outside, voices saying identifiable words. Were the other people ignoring them or could they tune them out completely, creating silence by concentrating? Not if the point was being present and aware. Surely then they'd hear the sounds more sharply than usual. He was thinking. What should he call this thought? Theorizing? Pondering? Back to the breath. A slight sensation of floating maybe caused by the stillness of his legs under him. He heard to his right someone's stomach gurgling, a very vivid digestive sound. It stopped. The best part of *Hamlet* was, in a way, that drifting stillness at the end when he lay dead on the stage. First the big, thrashing movements of the sword fight, then speaking his last words, getting quiet and small and focusing the entire audience's attention on his face, then dying in a cone of light from above. Bit more business. Horatio's speech. Final words. Silence. The clattering outbreak of applause like a rainstorm, the relief. He was missing that already and it had only been a few days. At the end of a job you thought you wanted freedom from the demanding hours and the way your life has been frozen in place for months but then immediately your days collapse into shapelessness. Henry noticed his posture was wilting. He straightened again. Control and order. Going on every night, firing out line after line, beat after beat, the same blocking, the same gestures pretty much. He knew by heart Hamlet's future at every moment and every word that had preceded. Such a contained feeling. Before and after were either side of him as he acted in the present moment, luminously detailed like a butterfly's wings. All that formation was now dissolved, the cast scattered. You could feel it happening in the final show party, the hugs and professions of love intensified by the knowledge that they were moving apart. It set in earlier, of course. A week or two before the end, news of jobs a few people had lined up would arrive. Envy and fear then fractured through the group; the brief shared culture—the habits and in-jokes, the affairs and the arguments—all coming to an end. Philip Townsend, a shameless, scene-stealing Polonius, had remained as expertly detached as ever, clear in his air of bitter amusement. Henry couldn't manage detachment or calm. Why else was he here, sitting on a cushion with these oddballs, staring at a wall and pretending to relax? He knew the answer. Everything was fine. Everything was going very well, in fact, but there was a shaking, a rattle in the engine, something small he couldn't identify, a persistent, anxiety-inducing tremor. One day, so the feeling went, it might just tear the whole fuselage open. Philip, the other side of a twelve-step program, devoted to his garden and the most astringent gossip, was calm. Henry was not and he wanted to be. Big things might be coming. He was being seen for something that would mean levelling up, a big role in the Marvel universe that would mean ridiculous money, personal assistant money, multiple homes money. He'd be everywhere, truly global, and he'd be gone, airlifted away. He wanted it badly, and he wanted it to happen before *The Beauty Part* hit the festival circuit and found distribution for its release. That was certainly part of the tremor, the feeling of dread it induced. He'd never felt right in the part. In the rushes, Henry had seen a mess, just destroyingly bad stuff, and he was now pretty sure that he was responsible for the first ever bad Miguel García movie. His American accent wasn't even up to it. He'd used a de-energized, throaty drawl to pass, a croaked whisper half the time, and had come out sounding like Hugh Laurie in *House*. Please God they find a decent performance to put together in editing. If not, he knew what would happen: the timer would start ticking down, the offers would dry up. He blamed his own inadequacies, obviously, but he blamed García, too. García might be a genius, but it wasn't obvious in what he said to actors. He hardly directed at all. It was like being back in the TV show, hitting your mark and spouting off. Henry and Sofie had worked out what to do for themselves while García, fat and unlikeable, sat low in his seat watching the screen and discussing things with his DOP. And the hunger, he'd almost forgotten the hunger through it all, how it made everything dim and grey, objects farther apart, how his concentration would suddenly break and the character would be gone from his body.

Henry felt an itch on his cheek, by his nose. He stopped himself reaching up to scratch. The itch intensified, fizzing, developing sharp edges that bit into his face. Henry breathed and waited and indeed it did begin to blur and fade. He didn't need to come here to find this out; it had happened a couple of times lying dead on the slope of the Barbican stage, following a drop of sweat rolling out of his hair. Shame Lucy wasn't here. When she'd recommended this place at the party he'd been in a coked-up rush of sincerity and exhilarated problem-solving. He could see her face now, the dark brows knitting, the uncertain eyes, saying, "I don't know. It works for me. It makes me just like calmer." She had made a downward gesture with an outspread hand in front of her body, to convey a settling of energy. She closed her eyes, becoming still and simple, and Henry loved her in that moment, was hollow with misery that the play was finally over and he was about to lose her, her tiny shoulders, her fierce frailty. And now here he was, doing as she'd said. Also, if you don't follow up on these brilliant ideas you have when high, they linger as a humiliation, a memory to wince at, and it comes to seem a stupid mistake ever to take yourself seriously. It had been a good party: the right amount of chaos and affection, though there'd been no sex. He wasn't sure why, he knew everyone too well maybe, or maybe Virginia. The image of Virginia, smiling and growing closer and caring for him, had been somewhere in his thoughts of meditation, exercise, perfect health and productivity. For a while now Henry had been thinking that they should try and be in the same city, and have a more regular life. How long had it been? More than a year of these occasional sprees together, without any commitment, keeping it light, keeping the party spirit going. Everything had been on hold for months because of the play, his life circling in one place. The day after the party, he had been disciplined about starting at things again, straightening out his flat, going for a run, putting in an Ocado order, writing emails, getting ready for the world. He wanted Virginia in it with him.

Straightening again. He hadn't noticed his posture going. The wall was drifting in front of him. He focused on a fleck in the paint, trying to get a grip and keep it still. It kept sliding then flicking back into place. He let it go again. How long was this going to go on for? Surely the walking was going to start soon. He should concentrate again on his breath but giving himself the instruction made him feel suddenly tired and sad. That was it: he was tired. With the realization, he felt the weight of his body on the ground, going nowhere. He wanted to close his eyes, to fall backwards onto the floor and sleep.

He would just have to wait until this was over. Henry sat still in the tank of his exhaustion. He had an interesting sensation of something draining from his head, a slow cold pouring. He sniffed, widened his eyes. While he was wondering if that sniff had been too loud, the bell was struck. Somehow, after all the waiting, the sound was unexpected, shockingly loud. Henry's heart raced. Everyone made the prayer gesture, palm to palm, bending forwards towards the wall, and stood up to walk. Henry did the same, uncrossing his legs and climbing up out of the discomfort he'd been ignoring. He felt it all now, a sour ache in his left knee, a numbness in the side of his left foot that start to tingle. He clasped his hands together as he'd been shown, his elbows jutting out at chest height. Another bell and the walking began. Henry thrust his right foot forward half a step and waited. The group moved so slowly that on his recovering legs Henry felt himself almost lose his balance. Thinking about walking, breaking it down into tiny mechanical components, was a hard way to walk. It didn't make much sense to Henry. The head in front of him belonged to a man. Smooth brown hair with two curved strands at the crown springing up into the air. Jutting ears. The chain of a necklace above his collar, the clasp off-centre, almost on his shoulder. Henry tried not to look. He remembered his nostrils and breathed. He slid his left foot forward along the mat. Virginia could move in with him, if she wanted, or they could get a new place together. It was time for a new place. He saw Virginia in a pleasing, indistinct interior, smiling, sprawling on a sofa, eating mouthfuls of salad leaves pinched together in her long fingers, walking through the place in her underwear. A real life. The end of loneliness. Why weren't they doing this? No more keeping it light, asking nothing. They could rescue each other. He saw them as children walking towards each other through the wreckage of success, miraculously unscathed. Some of the things she told him about her life. She'd told him about a friend of hers who had ended up on a yacht somewhere in the Adriatic or maybe even the Black Sea, a party of five or six, and things getting out of hand, usual scene but with a gun appearing and disappearing, too. And this was a businessman, an oligarch type, getting angry with anyone in his line of vision, not some sweet kid rapper messing around, swaggering around and shooting up into the night. An argument went on. Then this girl heard the engine start and someone said the phrase "international waters" and she freaked. Quietly she walked away from the group and climbed off the side of the boat. She swam for like half an hour back to the lights of the harbour. She heard shots fired, possibly— she didn't know—towards her. Then it's two in the morning and a model in a swimming costume and soaked shirt is walking barefoot through this town trying to find the cheap hotel she was staying in. She made it back, her feet a little cut up, showered and packed and went to the railway station immediately, waiting for dawn to head anywhere out of there on the first train. Virginia offered this as a funny story. Henry remembered her face after she'd told him. They'd been in a Japanese restaurant; with her chopsticks Virginia tweezered small amounts of translucent seaweed or black-eyed shrimps out of the lacquered compartments of a bento box as she told him. Half smiling, she waited for his reaction and Henry had the feeling she needed him to find it funny, to confirm that it was amusing, rather than miserable and awful. Henry had reached the end of the mat and now had to turn ninety degrees to the right. With which foot, inside or outside? How was this difficult? He shuffled around in a few small movements and stepped forwards again. He and Virginia had given each other permission to do whatever they wanted, to go where their chances took them, to whoever. Only now, in this room, he realized what they hadn't permitted each other, the right to care. Out of nowhere, Henry felt his arms grabbed, his elbows pulled up so that they were horizontal again. It was the robed instructor. He walked away again as though nothing had happened. Henry kept shunting his feet forwards and tried to overcome his annoyance at being singled out this way. He doubted his elbows had been drooping that much. He couldn't see where the instructor was now or whether anyone else was getting this treatment. Shocking, unfair, like being sucker-punched, but like a good pupil Henry brought his focus back to the breath in his nostrils. The bright, sharp chime of the bell: again it seemed to arrive too soon or too late, out of nowhere. They returned to their places, bowed again, sat. Henry gathered his legs into the sitting posture, reassembling the discomfort exactly as it had been before. Again the bell was rung, a softer splash of sound this time that smoothed away into the air. They were meditating again. This was taking a long time. Henry saw the emptiness of the next half-hour ahead of him. Nothing to do and nowhere to go. He named the thought. *Boredom*. He breathed in through his nose and out again. *Nose*, he though. *Boredom. Waiting.*

Bowing as he stepped over the wooden barrier to leave, stacking his cushion with the others, Henry thought that he hadn't achieved one moment of serenity or not thinking or whatever it was you were supposed to get out of this. Not a moment. At least, walking stiffly out, he felt a tiredness that might produce a good night's sleep. He glanced at others in the outer room, tying their shoes and swinging on their jackets. They all seemed satisfied, relieved in some way. Henry was about to walk down the stairs and slip out into his solitude when a voice said, "Excuse me. Hey." Here it comes, Henry thought: the reason he shouldn't have come. He turned to see one of the art school types he'd clocked earlier, a small man with pale skin and seventeenth-century facial hair, a short, pointed beard and horizontal moustache. "Yes?" Henry said. "What is it?"

"Oh, it's nothing. Sorry to bother you. It's just, Lucy texted and said you might come along. I just wondered if everything was okay for you?"

*

Another day. So much time to fill in this tiring city. Kristin decided to visit the theatre where *The Runaways* would be so that tomorrow she would know where she was going. She had already been to the Houses of Parliament that morning. She had taken photos of the intricate brown façade and the tall familiar British character that was Big Ben and his clock face. She had crossed Westminster Bridge—the water below flowing down towards Henry—to get a shot of the whole building over the Thames.

Now she was in a different part of London, out to the west, on a long street of regular white houses, quiet and geometric. Ahead, in the middle of the road on its own sort of island, was the pub that contained the theatre, a curved presence in all these straight lines of perspective. It had a green sign, a few empty benches outside, and windows that were decorated with white patterns of engraving: vases and strings between them. The door handle was a large brass sphere, the size of a baseball. The door was heavy as she pushed.

A drowsy afternoon inside, warm, beery, carpeted, sparsely populated. Music played in the background and was ignored, as in a clothes shop. A barman noticed Kristin come in, a young guy with a towel over one shoulder and his arms folded, two full sleeves of tattoos muddled together. He lifted his chin interrogatively. Could he help her?

Kristin felt obliged, now that she was there. She walked to the bar and asked for a glass of white wine. He offered her a choice. She asked for the chardonnay. He flipped an upturned glass the right way up, measured the wine into a metal cup and poured it in. It was a large measure. Kristin took it to a seat by the window and quietly set about drinking it away. She looked around. There was a sign for the theatre over a door. After a while, when the barman was out of sight, she got up and walked through it, finding herself a little soft and imprecise and lighthearted.

Beyond the door were stairs that led up to a closed ticket kiosk and then what must have been the theatre itself beyond open double doors. There were voices inside and lights clicking on and off. Kristin approached quietly and looked in. There were people on the stage in Victorian costumes, holding bundles of papers—scripts. They weren't acting or saying anything. They seemed to be waiting. Out of the near darkness a voice said, "Hello." A man was standing just inside the door, writing something in a small leather-bound notebook with a hanging tassel.

"Oh, I'm sorry, I just was passing."

"Can I help you?"

"No. I just wandered in. I'm coming tomorrow, you see. I'm excited to see the play."

"Hang on a moment." He stepped outside into the hall and pulled the doors closed after him.

"Are you? You look like Jeremy Banks, the writer."

"I am. How did you know?"

"I've seen your picture online. In *The Stage*, in that interview."

"You read *The Stage* in America?"

"Not really. No, I'm just particularly interested in the play."

"In the Brownings? Are you a scholar? It's a very long way to come just to see my play."

"Sure I'm interested in the Brownings. It's one of the reasons I'm here."

"Well, that's very flattering. If you hadn't already bought your ticket I would be inclined to give you a comp."

He ran a hand over the untidy lengths of hair that covered his baldness.

"Don't they need you in there?"

"Not right now. It's the tech. I'm observing mostly."

He looked a bit like a squared-off and heavy Henry but only the eyes were really reminiscent, deeply set, densely coloured, with that look of knowledge and kindness and imagination. Would Henry develop those tufty eyebrows too once he was older?

"Must be so exciting for you. Your first play."

"First one to make it this far."

Henry looked more like his mother. Kristin had worked that out from a photo of her she'd found online, taken in the nineties by the look of it, a portrait of her when she was singing: a velvet, off-the-shoulder dress, long, smoothly brushed hair, a sweet smile, that old-fashioned, virginal, demure sexiness that was the look for classical musicians. She was beautiful. Her looks revealed how feminine Henry's beauty was, in a way, tender and delicate.

"Poetry is what it's all about, isn't it?" Kristin said.

"Well, quite. More popular in America than I'd expected, the Brownings. I've had quite a few emails back and forth with a lady professor in California."

"I can believe it. I'm sorry to disturb you, sir. I must let you get back."

"No need to call me 'sir.' Really." He smiled at her. "What's your name?"

"Kristin."

"Kristin. Lovely. I'll look out for you tomorrow in the crowd."

"Sure. I'll be there."

*

Dinner would be Henry's treat but the choice of restaurant was his father's. He insisted on the usual place, the little Italian he had "discovered" sometime in the early eighties and where he'd gone on all his trips to London since. Henry's father would recommend it to other people in the village if he heard that they were going to London, his attitude in those moments worldly, patronizing, generous. He didn't look very worldly now, walking with Henry's mother up the Strand towards Aldwych where Giovanni's lurked beneath a red awning. Following behind his parents, Henry felt an unusual emotion, a rush of pitying love for them. In this environment, the fast, indifferent street, they looked old, buffeted and uncertain. They lacked the agility and sharpened peripheral vision of Londoners. People swerved around them. Henry, with his baseball cap pulled low, shepherded them towards their meal. He was committed to a good, friendly evening, the family united in general triumph, Hamlet achieved and his father's play, of all absurd things, about to open in a fringe venue.

Inside Giovanni's nothing had changed. Henry remembered it all from his previous visits, the heavily starched tablecloths, the straggling pot plants hanging from hooks on the ceiling, the silence without music, the old waiter in black waistcoat and patent leather slip-on shoes. Henry's father greeted him. "Good evening. Angelo, isn't it? You see. Good memory I've got. Table for three. Name of Banks."

The waiter gave no sign of recognizing Henry's father. His face was heavy, a pallid yellow after years away from the Italian sun. Short eyelashes and raised brows, large orbits around his eyes, gave him a disinterested look. When he wasn't required, Henry remembered, he had a spot by the cash register where he would stand and stare out of the window at the street. He led them to a table. Henry sat down. There was that poster of the Amalfi coast on the wall opposite: a whitewashed wall with a pot of red geraniums on top, a view of blue water bearing a white sailing boat that tilted to the right. The waiter handed them red leather menus.

Six other people had found their way into this fading establishment. An elderly couple sat in one corner. At another table there was a family of four, one child kicking his little legs and digging his fork into a bowl of ravioli, an older boy suffering the distortions of early adolescence, a fuzz of hair down the back of his neck, his facial features large and shining, his shoulders narrow and tense. He looked around as though startled when Henry's father loudly announced to the waiter, "Very good. We'd like a carafe of water and a bottle of your Valpolicella, thank you."

"You don't want a prosecco or champagne?" Henry asked. "This is all on me and I thought we were celebrating."

"Let's not get ahead of ourselves. Show hasn't opened yet."

"But it's happening. And mine has closed. Whatever you prefer."

164

"Champagne?" the waiter asked hopefully.

"No, no. The Valpolicella will be fine."

The waiter walked away.

Henry's mother spoke while reading her menu. "I'm not sure I want to drink too much. Really affects my sleep these days."

"I'll drink with you," Henry offered.

"I'm sure you will, Hen."

"What are you going to have?" his mother asked. "For food?"

Henry's father said, "I'll have what I always have here. The veal *scallopini* in Marsala. This place is known for it. Isn't that right?"

The waiter was back already with the wine. He twisted the corkscrew in and said. "The veal is very good. I can recommend." He drew out the stained cork and poured a measure of wine for Henry's father to approve. He did. "Excellent," he said, and the waiter poured. "None for the lady," he added.

"I didn't say none. Half a glass for me."

Henry looked at his mother. She, who said the least, somehow always set the mood. In her silent reactions it was determined whether you were allowed to enjoy yourself. Henry wanted normal family happiness, normal conviviality. He would stay in good humour and force his parents to do the same. He ran his eye down the menu of familiar classics, *insalata tricolore, prosciutto* and *melone*, seafood risotto, *puttanesca, arrabiata, carbonara, alle vongole, bistecca alla Fiorentina.* He slapped it shut.

"I'll have the veal also," he said.

"Oh, are we ordering now?" his mother asked. "I'm not quite ready yet."

"If you could give us a minute or two," his father said to the waiter, who nodded and set down the bottle before returning to his post by the cash register.

"Well then," Henry said, raising his glass. "Here's to us."

"Yes, why not?" his father said.

They chimed glasses. They drank.

"Woof," Henry said. "Tastes like red wine, I suppose."

"Are you going to be a snob?"

"Not at all. I said it tastes like red wine."

"Not good enough for you? Not up to celebrity standards?"

"Don't use the c-word, please. I'm an actor."

A clatter of fall. The adolescent at the other table had dropped his fork and now was straining down towards the carpet to retrieve it. The boy's father raised a hand to summon the waiter. "Could we get a new fork over here?" Americans. "It's okay," the boy said, upright again, holding the fork. "It's not okay. You can't eat with that. We'll get a new one."

This interruption, watched by Henry and his parents, reset their own conversation. They turned back to each other with indifferent faces.

"So," Henry began again. "How's the show looking?"

Henry's father proceeded to tell him at length, pausing only while he called the waiter over to place their order, his comments and complaints flowing around this obstacle like a river around a rock. Henry tried to offer advice from his professional experience but his father didn't seem to want it. His mother poured herself another half-glass of wine. "You could have just had a whole glass to begin with," Henry said lightly, smiling as though he'd made a joke. "But I didn't know I wanted it," his mother answered. Henry nodded and took a sip from his own glass. He was starting to feel the usual loneliness and defeat as he faced the wall of his parents. Such hard work. He very much wanted to take his phone out of his pocket for relief, to run some colour and light through his brain. He wanted in particular to check for a new email in the thread titled MARVEL PROJECT. There could be news.

"Even despite all that," his father said, "I just hope we get some press in."

"You will," Henry said. "That venue's shows are always reviewed. *The Stage* will review it. *Time Out*. The *Standard*. What you have to hope is that they review it well."

"Says he who got all raves for *Hamlet*."

"Well, almost all," said his mother.

At that moment, their veal arrived. Ovals of meat under a sheeny brown sauce accompanied by smaller ovals of fried potatoes. The waiter returned with a bowl of spinach and ricotta ravioli for Henry's mother. The obligatory moment with the grater and falling shavings of parmesan, the pepper, and then the pepper grinder carried away under the waiter's arm.

"Any developments in your glittering career?" Henry's mother asked as she unrolled her knife and fork from her napkin.

"Maybe. Something big. Bigger than previous things, I mean."

"Oh, really?" His father, sawing at his meat, looked directly at Henry.

"Yes. I actually can't talk about it too much."

"Nobody's forcing you."

"It's a movie thing. A superhero. Several movies probably."

"Like a cartoon?" his mother asked. "A children's film?"

"Not exactly. Lots of special effects, though."

167

"Very noisy, I imagine," his mother said.

"A commercial rather than artistic decision," his father said. "And why not?"

Henry sat back in his chair and sighed. He adjusted the angle of his cap, staring at the blue water of the Amalfi coast, the angled white sail.

He sat forwards again, returning to his food. "This veal is really good," he said. "You're absolutely right. No wonder this place is so well known for it."

"I know. Mine's delicious."

"I'm being ironic. Mine's like flipping shoe leather. I think the sauce is to hide their shame."

"I don't know what you're talking about."

"You're right. It's wonderful."

"Did you show Henry the photos Julian sent?" Henry's mother asked.

"Not yet. Hang on." Henry's father reached into his breast pocket for his phone. He tapped the screen a few times, swiped, swiped, and handed it across the table. "They made that sign themselves," his father said, reaching for his wineglass.

Henry's brother Julian had two children with his Chinese wife, Mei. Their English names were Milo and Chloë. In a living room in faraway Hong Kong Milo and Chloë held up a piece of paper on which they had painted *Congratulations Grandpa! Break a leg!!* A rainbow of three colours curved over the words. Glitter encrusted the top of the page.

"Aren't they beautiful?" Henry's mother asked.

They were. They had that refined, intelligent-looking beauty of Anglo-Chinese children, dark eyes, sweetly geometric hair. There were two pictures, one in which they both looked serious and one in which

Chloë's head had tipped back and she was laughing, showing her tiny teeth.

"Very cute," Henry said, handing back the phone.

Henry's father looked at the screen again and smiled at it before returning the phone to his pocket. Both of his parents were silent, deliberately it seemed, giving Henry a moment to consider what he wasn't, what he didn't have.

Henry took another sip of wine. "You asked me if I could bring my agent," he said. "I think I can get her to come."

"Oh, really?" His father looked up. "Well, that would be splendid."

In a taxi heading home, Henry took out his phone and texted Virginia. *Hey, you. Where are you? I'm missing you. When will I see you again? Too long, baby, too long.* He hit send and the message went with a whoosh. Henry looked out at the street.

Back in his flat, Henry checked his phone. Nothing. In bed, the clock reading 11:46, he looked again. Still nothing. Nothing again at 4:13 when he woke up for no reason. He looked again when he woke up properly at 10:11. Nothing.

*

The sight of Henry standing there, right by the door, looking at his phone while people filed past him into the theatre, broke Kristin's step. She was seized with the urge to turn back but pushed forwards, making her foot land, continuing. He was taller than she'd remembered. He wore tight, narrow trousers that made his legs seem to sway backwards at the knee. She looked down, avoiding his face. His shoes were clean Nike trainers made of some futuristic grey mesh. She walked past him—she had to—and looked up at his face, the stubble on his cheek, the curve of his nostril. He didn't notice. Kristin showed her ticket to the person on the door. She went in. He hadn't looked up but he must have felt her going past, the reunion starting to happen. She found a seat, put her handbag underneath it, settled her dress over her thighs, neatened her bangs. She felt a sliding drop of sweat between her shoulder blades like a cold fingertip. She would smell humid and human if she wasn't careful, the shampoo sweating out of her scalp. Seats filled. Henry's father appeared and scanned the audience, his face several times breaking into a large smile as he waved at someone known, before he sat down in the front row. Kristin tried waving at him but wasn't sure he saw. Henry entered, sliding his phone into his pocket, and sat on the end of the front row with his legs outstretched, crossed at the ankle.

The play began. Kristin found it hard to take in at first. The theatre was so small and the actors so close it seemed ridiculous they had to pretend not to see the audience a few feet away. The actors' costumes were heavy, meant for much colder rooms, and their hairstyles absurd. Robert Browning had large, brushy sidewhiskers. Elizabeth Barrett's hair was parted severely in the middle and drooped down on either side of a white line of scalp. When they sang their voices were so loud and earnest, they almost hurt. The actors' faces yawned and bulged. Kristin could see clear bumps of sweat on Robert Browning's forehead. There was a lot of writing, letters delivered to and fro across the stage, scenes of candlelight and excited reading and scratching quill pens, inspiration. How fitting this was. Kristin knew exactly what the characters were feeling, how you could pour your heart into a letter. They spoke a language of love that sounded old-fashioned but everyone knew it, everyone would speak it if they were brave enough. Enamoured. Beloved. Betrothed. Beseech. Afeared. Ought. Nought. Anew. When Robert and Elizabeth ran away together, they had to sit beside one another on two seats and sway while through the speakers came the sound of rumbling carriage wheels and horses' hooves. They held hands and raced into their fate. The stage went black. During the applause, the actors got up and walked off, a human shifting in the darkness.

The intermission was wasted on one visit to the bathroom. Kristin needed to relieve herself and check her appearance. A long wait in a corridor preceded an unpleasant tiled bathroom, a toilet with a splashed seat that needed cleaning, and the redness of someone's period at the bottom of the bowl. In the mirror after, Kristin found her own eyes beseeching her, large and wild with tiredness during this important evening, but there was nothing she could do.

The songs and action of the second half began with terrible challenges to their marriage, the light of a single candle, the sound of heavy rain, and led on to happiness and literary triumph in Italy, represented with a lighting effect of golden sunlight through leaves and birds twittering through the speakers. Kristin was very happy for the lovers, for the message it was spreading through the audience, through Henry's brain as he sat there in the front row, but when the play ended and applause broke out, Kristin felt fear. She applauded, raising her hands up over her head when Henry's father was beckoned onto the stage. In the noise, she could moan to herself, "Oh no, no, no, oh no," and no one heard.

It was over. The lights were back on. People standing, murmuring, shuffling. Kristin stood up. Her hands flew about her body, fixing her hair, straightening her dress, one fingertip cleaning the corners of her mouth. Henry was already through the door. The remainder of the crowd had to move slowly, filtering out in ones and twos. Once out, it was down to the pub, descending the stairs one by one. Kristin had time to look around. She felt the urge to use her hands to tidy the whole place. She noticed the shabbiness of the carpet, the handprints on the rail, the dust on the glass in the door. She wanted to vacuum, to spray and polish and cleanse and make everything perfect. Meanwhile, nothing was ready and she was processed down the stairs, trapped behind the people in front of her, with others waiting behind.

The audience accumulated at the bar—those who weren't leaving right away—and added to the crowd already in the pub. Kristin couldn't think what to do except join the queue for the moment and wait to order a glass of white wine. She took a bill out of her purse and held it in her hand, ready. She put it in the barman's hand. She received her heavy change, the large golden glass of wine. She sipped and had the same sweet-cold taste in her mouth as yesterday. She tipped her head back and took a large swallow. She looked around and saw Henry's mother on the edge of a small group of people, smiling but not talking. Kristin recognized her from the photograph. Older, less colourful, with the same straight-backed poise. Her hair had faded like the fabric of a chair that caught the sun; there was Henry's beauty all right but aging, unfastened, dissolving, flowing away into time. Somehow, this trance of appreciation, Kristin's deep knowledge of Henry Banks and his family, meant that when she caught sight of Henry she started towards him without hesitation. He was talking to a woman. Her face was hidden by a sharp hairstyle, but Kristin recognized his agent from the street, the woman with the hard eyes and the vape pen. Kristin turned immediately and almost into the chest of Henry's father. Kristin swung her glass out of the way.

Henry's father said loudly, over the noise of the bar, "Aha, it's my American fan. Did you enjoy the show?"

"I did. I thought it was wonderful. It's ... it's ... I don't know what to say. It's amazing that you wrote all those songs."

"You liked them, did you?" Red wine tilted in his glass.

"I did." Kristin wasn't sure what to say next. "I thought they were just great. Such a talented family."

"Ah, and here he is." Henry's father landed a heavy hand of affection on the shoulder of the man who had played Browning as he walked past. The man stopped and sighed, drooping forwards. His cheeks were angrily red where his sideburns had been unglued. He looked strange in soft, modern clothes. "Hello, Jeremy," the actor said, his voice quiet and rasping, tired. "How was that? Not too bad? I think we got away with it. Couple of moments in the first half, but."

"It was splendid. I'm very pleased. Really. Just terrific. Isn't that right?" Henry's father called on Kristin as a witness.

"I loved it," she said. "You have a beautiful voice. It's such a gift."

"That's very kind of you to say." The actor closed his eyes for a second and tilted forwards in an abbreviated bow. "Can I get anyone anything?" he said, upright again, pointing at their glasses.

"We're fine," Henry's father said. "Off you go." As the actor set off towards the bar, Henry's father turned back to Kristin and said, "Such sensitive flowers, these

performers. I spend my life surrounded by them."
Raising his voice, he said, "And here's another one." It
was Henry. Kristin looked at him, looked around. She
didn't see the agent. She saw the door closing and, she
thought, the agent in the street. Henry's father said to
Henry, "This is Kristin. We met the other day. Would
you believe she's come all the way from America to see
my play? What do you think of that?"

"I think I'm shocked," Henry said. "Is that true?"

Henry was speaking to her, looking at her. She man-
aged to say, "Not just for that."

"Well, I'm amazed." Henry turned an amused
expression slowly back to his father.

"You seem very cheerful. Everything all right?"

"I'm very well. Just had some good news, I think."

"Oh, yes? About that cartoon?"

"Something like that."

"Well, good for you. We'll talk about it some other
time. Do excuse me. Right now there's someone I really
must speak to who has come up from Hampshire. Not
quite the same distance." Kristin watched him step away
and greet a friend, a short man of a similar age wearing
a burgundy sweater. This man put his fists on his hips,
tilted his head to one side and said, "Well, well, well."

It was hard to turn away and look again at Henry.
She knew too clearly what was happening and this realization kept repeating as they talked, a kind of doub-
ling in the moment, a thumping as her mind confirmed
and everything in the room arrived inside itself again
and again. She could feel the blood in her fingers, her
hot breath escaping. Henry asked if she'd really come
all the way from America to see this play and she said
no, not really. She had come for a lot of things. Henry

didn't seem to be recognizing her. She said something about Buckingham Palace and the butterfly exhibit that she really wanted to see. She needed to moisten her mouth. There was a kind of clicking in her throat, her dry tongue lumbering as she spoke. She said that she'd come to see him, too, that she'd been at *Hamlet* for the last night, and she took a sip of wine. "You were there? That wasn't an easy ticket to get."

"I know," she said. "It cost me a lot of money." He smiled at her. She looked up at him, fully into his eyes, and everything was fine, a great warmth and pliancy flooded her body. This was the moment they were reunited. His expression changed very slightly. A question appeared in it. She answered in the way she looked back. His smile brightened with amusement and confidence. He put a hand on her arm and leaned towards her and said, "I'm going to get myself a drink. I'm not planning to stay much longer. How about you?"

"I'll do whatever you want to."

Henry laughed, making Kristin's heart jump. His face changed. He said, "You see that person behind you taking a photo of his friend?" Kristin turned, saw. "He's actually taking a photo of me in the background. You can see by the angle. I bet if you checked his zoom. I'm not sure I want to stick around for much more of this."

"We should get out of here."

"It'll be on Instagram in like two minutes. We should go somewhere and celebrate."

The first time they were outside together in the open air, their voices freshly audible, intimate.

The first time he called her by her name.

The first time they got into a car together, one he'd ordered on his phone.

London, those long hard streets so laborious to cross, was now a gloss and glide of coloured light outside the windows. The warm weight of Henry's hand was on her thigh.

Kristin would rather have gone to his place by the river where she would have seen his possessions and been folded into his life and they would have had a view of the river but Henry said that he wanted to go to hers. Such an insane feeling, walking up the creaking carpeted stairs with Henry Banks at her side, his hand on the back of her neck. He seemed too real, too large for the place. When they went into her tiny room, he was so powerful, so forceful. He lifted her hips right up off the bed as he removed her underwear. All that time spent imagining herself into the future, living several steps ahead of herself, and now she felt like she couldn't keep up. She wanted to hold on to the taste of his skin, to keep the stabilizing weight of him on top of her. With one forearm under her neck, gripping her left breast in his hand, his breath blasted into her ear. He was very fierce. She didn't have time to feel all her sensations before he was out of her again. He finished mostly on her belly, scattering up in warm droplets also over her heart. He pushed himself backwards onto his feet and walked into the tiny bathroom. He returned with a loose rosette of toilet paper. "There we are," he joked, "all better," and wiped her with it. He returned to the bathroom, where she heard him drop the paper into the toilet and then the drumming of his long urination down onto it. She lay still, looking up at the red light on the white box of the smoke detector. When Henry returned, he leaned down over her to pick up his shirt. He let her kiss him softly on the neck but didn't respond in kind. "I'm going to head off," he said. He squirmed his feet back into his new trainers without adjusting the laces. "Don't. Let me look at you," he said. Kristin had folded her arms across her breasts and he meant for her to put them back down by her sides. She remembered that later, the moment of obeying, putting her arms back down, so that he could give her a brief, calm, smiling inspection. "You don't have my number," she said. Now he met her eyes. "No," he said, "but I know where you are. Don't worry."

"Don't go," she said. "I need to talk to you."

"It's late," he said, putting on his jacket. "I have to get up for something. I'm sorry. Crazy timing." And he left.

*

How could anyone ever give up smoking when you can retrieve so much of yourself in that small, deliberate action: the packet, the neat, dry feeling of the paper cylinder, the snap or scrape of making a flame, the relief of inhaling. Henry sat on his balcony, regretting his evening. At night the wind was still cold. He made a fist of his free hand and stuck it in his jacket pocket. He was the shaking in the machine. He was asking for trouble. If she hadn't looked up at him in that way, he wouldn't have done it. Those soft, widening eyes: a look of infinite fuckability. She had had an effect on him and he'd allowed himself the impulse. Also, of course, he wanted to escape into her adulation of him, away from his parents, his father trying to make use of him to impress other people. Or having to confront those actors. The play came back to Henry's mind in flashes of boisterous absurdity, the actors gripping each other's forearms and singing into each other's faces, sparks of spittle flying. One thing Henry could say for himself was that he could act. On stage, playing Hamlet, he knew what he was doing. He had known.

And now, according to his agent, he was a few negoti-ated clauses away from a whole new level. Henry would be back in the zoo for good. The zoo was how Henry had come to think of the shared, gated world of the famous. In there, you knew what you were looking at. You recog-nized the inhabitants, a lion, a giraffe, a chimp, and if you didn't know who they were, one of the many zookeep-ers, the publicist, agents, producers, would be there to tell you. He would be safe in there with the other animals, fed and watered and fêted beyond the velvet rope.

Henry saw himself in the costume, caped, masked, muscled, standing on the edge of a tall building with weather behind him. He saw himself leaning forwards, seeming to fall but fearless, expressionless, until he is horizontal and starts to fly.

He hadn't told Virginia yet. He stretched backwards to extract his phone from his trouser pocket and send her a message. He'd been stupid, this evening. Avoiding the actors, avoiding his parents, he'd found an easy diversion in Kristin, an acceptable if pointless lay. And she was odd, too, that woman. What was she going on about visiting a butterfly sanctuary together? And she seemed to think they'd met before or something. But what time zone was Virginia in right now, east or west? And who knew what the fuck she was up to. Henry found out now. Finally, she had sent him a reply. *Hey, hon. So many messages. I'm just hours away. Have been in Germany. Will explain soon. Early flight to London!*

*

When Kristin awoke she pulled up her t-shirt and found the silvery tightness of Henry still on her skin. Without seeing that, she might not have believed it had happened, though the air of the room still felt disturbed and the shocked mirror and mute smoke alarm seemed to remember.

Why had he gone? She hadn't said anything that would drive him away. She couldn't remember everything she'd said to him but it wouldn't be that. More likely, she hadn't said enough. He had looked ignorant still when he left, like he hadn't realized or remembered. He had to get up for something. That's what he'd said and that was all it was. He had an early appointment. Fine. She would get up and go to his place and wait. There wasn't even any hurry. They were lovers now. It was all happening. Kristin hadn't yet had the chance to make him feel wonderful and sensual in the ways she had imagined but that would come.

By now, there was a warm familiarity about the breakfast room, and this morning it seemed to Kristin to have a particularly comfortable, cat-like calm, softly folded, drowsing. She ordered again her poached eggs and coffee and ate in silence.

Either side of the underground journey was a beautiful spring day pieced together from small, tender elements, clouds, dashes of sunlight, shaking leaves, the clap of pigeons in flight, a delicate, playful, hair-lifting breeze. The river, sliding low between its banks, was patched with melting blue and brown. Rising forms of glass and brick all shone. She walked along the route still clear in her memory. When she expected it to, the turn to the right appeared and she walked straight to the front door of his building and pressed the button by his printed name. Nothing. She pressed again. Nothing. She was backing away to look up at the building when a man passed her heading to the door. He swiped in with a key card and Kristin followed. He looked back at her as she caught the closing door and entered behind him. She gave him a smile of vacuous, everyday innocence, which he seemed to accept, and she started up the stairs. Fortunately, he lived on the ground floor and did not follow her up to see her stopping outside number five with no key, unable to go in.

Kristin tried to look in through the spyhole but couldn't make anything out beyond a bulge of white light, bending shapes that must be walls, ceiling and floor. Henry's protected and secret world that she was about to share. She took off her backpack and slid down the wall until she was sitting with her knees by her chin. Maybe this afternoon they could go to the butterfly exhibit together.

Kristin waited an unknown, unconscious amount of time. The numbers on her watch couldn't comment on it, speaking their unfriendly, public language. She sat still as a seed. Betrothed. Beloved. Ought. Nought. The quiet of the hallway gathered close around her heartbeats. It flew apart with the metallic scraping of the lock downstairs, the click of the door, the rush of outside sound. Kristin got quickly to her feet.

Henry's face changed twice when he saw her, once disarranged with confusion and then hardening with certainty. He held a small suitcase in one hand. Behind him was a woman, thin and tall. Henry said, "How did you get in here?"

"I just came."

"What do you mean you just came? How do you even know where I live?"

The woman said, "Henry, what's going on here? Who is this person?" She had an American accent, just like Kristin's.

"It's fine. It's nothing to worry about."

"Henry, let's not get hung up on how I got here. I'm here. That's what matters."

"This is not cool. This is not okay. You shouldn't …"

"Don't say that. Don't say that. Don't say that. Of course you should. We're meant to be together. You remember me, you just don't remember. We met. At the airport, like a year and a half ago. We talked about this."

"Fuck me. I don't even know your name to get a restraining order."

The woman giggled, "Oh my God, is this like a full-on stalker situation?"

Kristin told her, "No," then ignored her. "But you're wrong. In your heart of hearts …"

"Don't come any closer to me."

Kristin didn't realize that she was walking towards him and she didn't stop. Henry shot out his arm and hit the knob of her shoulder with the flat of his hand. The straight force of the impact shocked tears into her eyes. It felt like pure hatred. "Just go. Keep going," he said. "Don't come back. Seriously now." Kristin couldn't control her face—her mouth was open and she couldn't shut it.

She ran past Henry, past the woman, and down the stairs.

"Hey!" he shouted, as though maybe he'd realized his mistake and was about to say something else. She stopped and looked up as her bag flew towards her and hit her also, just below her left knee.

Henry's blows had knocked the substance from Kristin's body. Light as air, she could feel nothing except the breaking in her chest. Her heart was breaking. She felt it go, the unbearable pain of splitting and scattering, the burning new emptiness at her centre.

How could Henry have been so wrong? How could he not have known? And who was that ugly, laughing person?

In the moment of these questions, Kristin could have been freed. She could have figured out a better ending and escaped. But she didn't. Instead, she saw what she would do. There were even stairs to make it easy. A simple solution: she wanted to put out the fire of pain; she wanted always to be by Henry.

Strange that there was not more of a barrier or divide. At the bottom of the steps was a narrow margin of gritty dirt and then the water. The water covered her shoes, was up to her knees. She felt an intimate sensation of exposure, like a dream of being naked in public. When she was fully in she wished she had worn her dress again instead of her trousers, heavy and wrapping, loosely swaddling. Wearing her dress, she would have floated and billowed. It would have spread beside her like butterfly wings as she met a more mystical death. Instead, there were these strange British voices shouting behind her, heard clearly in the breaks in the hard work of getting her head under the shockingly cold water and keeping it there. When it was under, she had to persuade herself to breathe in. She had time to think that she should have written Henry a final letter so that he would properly understand and could grieve. She remembered—distantly, fondly—the breathable air over her head, above the surface of the water.

She thought of the airport, of all the people moving as usual, and her name being called for her flight home and no one answering.

DREAM SEQUENCE

"Adam Foulds is a young British novelist of striking talent and eclecticism. His style is first-rate, combining precision with a rich poetic imagination. He is able to do more with language, and at greater depth, than most other British novelists of his generation."

—Andrew Holgate, *The Sunday Times*

"On the level of the sentence, there's much to admire in this novel. Foulds has a searching eye for detail and an apparently helpless compulsion to wring imagery from his subject."

—Tim Martin, *The Telegraph*

"Foulds writes like no one else; while individual scenes are rendered with poetic simplicity, they fit together into an elliptical, complex plot readers will puzzle over long after finishing this novel."

—*Kirkus Reviews*

"Combining careful, considered prose with horrific realism, the latest from Foulds expertly renders the Allied campaigns in Italy and North Africa during WWII ... readers will be amazed at this deeply felt, vivid novel."

—*Publishers Weekly* (Pick of the Week)

Acknowledgements

I am indebted to Robin Robertson, Michal Shavit, Sarah Chalfant, and Paul Prescott for invaluable advice and support during the writing of *Dream Sequence*. I would like once again to express my gratitude to Beatrice Monti della Corte for time spent at the Santa Maddalena Foundation and for her friendship.

The name of one of the characters in this book belongs to a bidder at an "immortality auction" held on behalf of Freedom From Torture, a charitable organization dedicated to the treatment, rehabilitation, and legal support of victims of torture. They do extraordinary work. Further information can be found at freedomfromtorture.org where donations can also be made.